D1530881

ESPECIALLY FOR GIRLS™
presents

THE RIGHT KIND OF GUY

by

Sheary Suiter

TEMPO BOOKS, NEW YORK

This book is a presentation of
Especially for Girls™
Weekly Reader Books.

Weekly Reader Books offers book clubs
for children from preschool through high school.

For further information write to:
Weekly Reader Books
4343 Equity Drive
Columbus, Ohio 43228

Especially for Girls™
is a trademark of Weekly Reader Books.

THE RIGHT KIND OF GUY

A Tempo Book/published by arrangement with
the author

PRINTING HISTORY
Tempo Original/September 1985

All rights reserved.
Copyright © 1985 by Sheary S. Suiter
This book may not be reproduced in whole or in part,
by mimeograph or any other means, without permission.
For information address. The Berkley Publishing Group,
200 Madison Avenue, New York, New York 10016.

ISBN: 0-441-72382-9

"Caprice" and the stylized Caprice logo are trademarks
belonging to The Berkley Publishing Group

Tempo Books are published by The Berkley Publishing Group,
200 Madison Avenue, New York, New York 10016.
Tempo Books are registered in the United States Patent Office.
PRINTED IN THE UNITED STATES OF AMERICA

1

I pushed my way through the heavy glass doors of Ridgeway High's cafeteria and rushed over to the far side of the room where Brenda Jackson sat waiting for me at our usual table.

"Glad you could make it, Williams," my best friend called out.

I knew that she intended for me, and half the lunch room as well, to detect the more than slight degree of sarcasm in her voice. Bren hates to wait for anyone or anything, even though she herself is notorious for being late.

"I grabbed a piece of chocolate cake for you," she continued, her tone still reprimanding. "They were going fast."

Bren knows that chocolate anything is my downfall; of course, Bren knows me better than anyone alive. We first met the summer Dad and I moved to Alaska, right after Mom died. At that time, Bren had come up to me with that wide, toothpaste-commercial grin of hers, saying "Hi, Maggie, I'm Bren. I live just down the street." That was two years ago and we've been friends ever since.

"Thanks for the cake, Bren, but really, it's not my fault I'm so late," I said, pleading my case. "Actually, I made record time, considering Mrs. Mansing didn't even let us come inside until ten minutes into shower time."

She gave me one of her "Oh, sure" looks, handed me the cake, and turned her attention back to her own half-empty lunch tray. I dropped my books on the bench opposite hers and headed for the lunch line.

P.E. right in the middle of the day is *not* my idea of an ideal schedule. Especially when you have an instructor like Mrs. Mansing who believes in holding class outdoors just as soon as the winter's snows have turned to a slushy muck and mud known to Alaskans as "break-up."

All over Anchorage everyone was cheering each other with predictions of an early spring. But all it meant to me and the other girls in Mrs. Mansing's class was that we got the privilege of enjoying track and field exercises in the cold of mid-March instead of early April. To top it off, track and field happens to be one of my least favorite sports, since my short little legs provide me with an automatic handicap.

At least P.E. falls just before my lunch period, so if I need some extra primping time (and I *always* need extra primping time), I can steal it from my stomach.

Missing a meal now and then doesn't hurt me anyway. At 5'1", even a couple of extra pounds shows up too quickly.

As I reached the front of the hot-lunch line, the looks of the day's menu—overdone fish sticks, canned peas, instant mashed potatoes, and wilted green salad—made me consider simply replacing the main courses with an extra piece of chocolate cake. Contrary to Bren's warning, there were still some servings left.

Knowing me though, I'd be plagued with feelings of guilt all afternoon, so I went ahead and chose what the textbooks would call a square meal, somehow mustering up enough will power to pass by the dessert section, and joined Brenda.

"Actually I'm glad you're late," she chided. "You just missed seeing the new boy."

"New boy? What new boy?" I mumbled, stuffing my mouth with the gummy mashed potatoes so I could get to the cake.

"Ridgeway got a new boy today, a senior, and he's . . . TALL!" she said dreamily.

At 5'10", Bren places a premium on boys with height. If I ever get the opportunity to accept a date, that's one problem I won't have to worry about.

"Sounds like you already have designs on this guy," I said. "What about Randy?"

Bren had been dating Randy Thompson longer than she had gone out with anyone yet. Bren's the kind of girl who always has dates, but because she's prone to a new crush every week, she also has the reputation of being rather fickle-hearted.

"Oh, Randy's still around," she said in her overly casual voice that told me she still really was interested in him after all. "But ever since he joined that stupid club, he doesn't seem to have much time for me."

"You know he joined the Computer Club in self-defense," I reminded her, "because you're always so busy with Fashion Board activities. In fact, weren't you the one who encouraged him to find some outside interests?" *So he wouldn't find another, less busy girl friend?* I thought to myself.

Personally I understood how left out of Bren's life Randy could have felt at times. I'd been there.

Even though Bren is my best friend, sometimes I can't help resenting the fact that just because she'd inherited some genes that told her body to grow, she'd had the opportunity to try out for a position on the new teen Fashion Board begun last fall by Farland's Department Store.

Farland's has a reputation for being one of the few stores in town that always carries the latest fashions from "Outside," as we Alaskans refer to the other 49 states. So it's every girl's favorite place to shop for clothes and accessories.

Of course, Bren's good grades and outgoing personality, not to mention her huge blue eyes and glamorous blonde hair, all contributed to the fact that she'd won one of the ten much-coveted Board positions.

It took me a while to get used to the idea that her new position demanded a lot of her spare time. At first, I felt really left out. But gradually I managed to find ways to fill the hours when Bren was busy modeling in fashion shows or working in the store's Teen Department.

In the beginning, I tried calling up our other girl friends and going around with them. But they liked to hang out at the malls a lot, which is OK, but after four weekends in a row, I'd memorized every style in every color in every teen department in town.

I guess Dad must have noticed my moping, because that was about the time we went and picked out two roly-poly golden retriever puppies and brought them home.

But right now wasn't the time to let myself start thinking about our puppies, Cherub and Cookie, especially not about poor Cherub, so I pushed them to the back of my mind and said to Bren, "Besides the fact that he looks like a beanpole, what else do you know about this new boy? What's his name, anyway?"

Bren stuck her nose up in the air playfully, pretending great personal offense at the beanpole remark and answered, "His name is Matt Brennan, he just happens to be from your old hometown in Oregon, and, to serve you right, that's all you'll get out of me!"

Continuing her charade of the insulted friend, she swept up her lunch tray and headed for the drop-off counter.

I grabbed my own empty tray and ran after her.

"Come on, Bren, give me a break. You know I can't recognize all the *old* seniors on sight, let alone a new one."

Even though we're best friends, Brenda is a junior and I'm only a sophomore. That first summer when Dad and I had just moved to Anchorage so he could better pursue his geological research, she'd listened and sympathized when I'd had nobody else to talk to about my mother's death.

Somehow we didn't even realize until school registration that we were a grade apart and at first it was a real blow. But our friendship managed to survive the class rivalry and schedule differences that often pull friends of different ages apart. If anything, the struggle to overcome the artificial obstacles of an age difference brought us closer together—a fact I tried my best to remember on occasions such as these. Brenda could be so stubborn!

"Sorry, Williams, find your own man," she sang out as she marched off toward the foreign-language hall.

There really was no sense pursuing the subject, since when Bren got into one of her obstinate moods, forget trying to bully anything out of her; even begging wouldn't work.

But I tried anyway, pleading for just a single hint as I followed her down the hall. But she refused even to tell me the color of his hair. She claimed that once I spotted him, I'd try to steal him away.

As if they were going steady already!

I knew of course that he probably hadn't even spoken a word to her...yet. But she always liked to make believe I was some kind of femme fatale, even when we both knew I'd never even had a real date, let alone the ability to steal another girl's boyfriend.

Not that I didn't dream of becoming someone more glamorous. But brains, not beauty, always seemed to be my forte. I guess people usually try to live up to whatever's expected of them, and with two professors for parents, I always knew that Mom and Dad took it for granted that I'd pull above-average grades.

According to Mom, these expectations began early. She once told me that Dad used to read his geology books aloud to me before I was born!

Whether or not Dad's prenatal instruction had anything to do with it, I'm duly appreciative of the fact that studying always has been easy for me. But when it comes to interacting socially, especially if it involves a cute boy or a group of strangers, I always seem to act like a natural imbecile.

Specifically, whenever I become nervous or embarrassed, my tongue has this special talent of sticking relentlessly to the roof of my mouth so that I'm caught wordless.

It was only after Mom passed away that this problem became apparent, so when the affliction showed no sign of departing on its own, my father and the school counselor decided that I should enroll in Speech 101 this term. Their theory was that my desire to achieve a passing grade in Mrs. Sutherlin's class would override my unaccountable fright.

Suddenly I realized that I'd let a very important fact completely slip my mind.

"Bren! I just remembered I've got to give a speech next period. I meant to practice it during our lunch break." -

Unfailingly unsympathetic when it comes to my academic problems, probably because they occur so infrequently, she answered, "So? Why don't you just say it to me now?"

"Now? Here in the hallway with all the other kids around?" She had to be kidding.

"Why not? Can't you talk and walk at the same time? I notice you're doing a pretty good imitation of it right now."

Rather than reply with something less than ladylike, I gave her a very dirty look.

"Come on, Maggie. Hurry up, it's probably only five minutes until first bell."

Final bell rings a minute after the first warning bell, which meant I didn't have much time to waste.   -

So I took a deep breath and spoke for three minutes on the geological dynamics of earthquakes, compliments of my father's offer to help me choose a speech topic.

When I'd finished—after ignoring the weird looks kids gave me along the way—Bren said my speech was fine. A dull subject, but well-organized and well-presented. I hoped Mrs. Sutherlin would be as kind.

We were discussing Carol Conners' devastatingly gorgeous new perm when we arrived at Bren's Spanish class. Just as the obnoxious buzz of first bell sounded, Bren turned to me in an offhand manner and said, "By the way, Maggie, I almost forgot something too. At last night's Fashion Board meeting, Mrs. MacDonald announced that Farland's is bringing out a new spring line of apparel for Petites. So the store is creating another position on the Board."

I stopped dead in my tracks. I knew my friend was eating up the silly-looking, open-mouthed expression on my face, but I couldn't help over-reacting.

Still repaying me either for my being late or for the beanpole remark or both, she gave me a mischievous grin and added, "Yes, Williams, they want shorties!"

"But, Bren. . ." I stammered, beginning to comprehend my friend's implications.

"Sorry, Maggie, gotta run. You'd better get moving yourself. You're going to be late for your speech!" As Bren disappeared into her classroom, she promised, "I'll tell you all about it on our way home."

I stood there in the middle of the hallway with a stupid, dazed expression on my face, until finally I realized I was all alone and that the final bell would be ringing any second.

I spun around and raced back up the foreign-language hall. Speech class was only one hall away, but to get there first I had to go back out into the Commons area. I figured I still had a 50-50 chance at least of making it to the classroom door before the late bell.

And maybe I would have made it, if it weren't for the fact that I wasn't the only one racing to get to class on time. As I threw my weight against the right-hand side of the double doors that led to English hall, everything seemed to happen at once, so that even as I recognized Carol Conners' face (not as easy face to miss, I admit; a face any cheerleader or homecoming queen could envy), it was too late to prevent the disaster already in progress.

Someone on the other side of the door had a more forceful pull than my push. Losing my balance, I went flying forward, catapulting right into Carol. The two of us ended up sprawled across the hallway floor—notebooks, papers, and textbooks scattered everywhere.

The only survivor was Carol's companion, a tall boy with thick, dark hair and shining eyes, who stood a little distance back, looking down at the two of us with a charmingly crooked little smile on his lips.

Carol's face, however, showed not the slightest sign of amusement.

"Why don't you watch where you're going? You could have killed me with that door!" accused Carol.

I knew Carol didn't know me, didn't know my name, didn't care the slightest thing about me, but I didn't think it was fair of her to be so vehement. After all, it *had* been an accident!

"Hey, if this is anyone's fault, it's mine," interceded the boy. "I'm the one who opens doors on the wrong side of the aisle." He walked over and squatted down between Carol and me to help sort out papers. "I'm left-handed," he explained to me. "I often do things unconventionally."

Carol, too, was acting unconventionally, she wasn't saying a word. The three of us were busy sorting papers when the boy reached toward me with some notes in his hand and asked, "These yours?" Our eyes connected for a few extra seconds, jolting my insides with a shimmery shudder. Had the boy felt it too? Or was I imagining things?

I think Carol may have noticed something though, because she moved in a little closer and said, "I'd introduce her, Matt, but I'm afraid I don't know her name. She must be an underclassman." Dismissing the subject of introductions, she went on, "And since you're accepting all the blame for this fiasco, Matt, how about a little help over here?"

"Oh, Carol, are you always so serious?" he teased her. "I'll help you in a minute, I promise, just as soon as I've properly introduced myself to this underclassman friend of yours." Carol's only response was an indignant little lift of her well-shaped chin.

"Matt Brennan, new kid in school," he said to me, extending his hand.

"Maggie Williams."

I placed my hand limply into his firm, warm one and watched shyly as he pumped my arm up and down several times. Then I let go, but Matt's grip lingered and he seemed to free my hand a bit reluctantly.

Overcome with nervousness, I looked down at the floor. Then grabbing up the few remaining pages, I crammed them into my notebook, intent on escaping the uncomfortable situation.

Carol finished with her mess of papers at the same time. Looking at Matt as she stood up, she said, "If you still want me to show you the way to Mr. Masterson's class, we'd better get going."

"Gotta run," said Matt, as he gave me one last, quicksilvery smile and hustled off to join Carol. I hadn't even begun to unstick my tongue from the roof of my mouth.

Of course, the minute he was out of sight I realized that I must have seemed like a total and complete geek. Especially with Carol for comparison.

Yet I couldn't help going over and over every single minute of our brief encounter. I was still thinking about the strange feelings Matt evoked in me when I found myself at the door of my speech class without a plausible explanation for being tardy.

I wondered—would Mrs. Sutherlin possibly accept the excuse that I'd been too busy to notice the tardy bell? Too busy falling in love with a new boy named Matt Brennan?

2

When I walked into Mrs. Sutherlin's class, Harold Brenski stood behind the podium at the front of the class, already in the middle of his speech. From that I knew that I wasn't horribly late since Harold was always the first to volunteer. I admired his bravery, if nothing else about him.

Mrs. Sutherlin gave me a quizzical look as I slid into one of the back row seats. I lifted my shoulders and gave her a sheepish look that meant, "Sorry!" At least I wouldn't have to do any explaining until after class.

When Harold finished his speech on "Alaskan Aviation" (tell me, who really cares that Alaska holds the record for private pilots per capita, or that Lake Hood sets new records for float plane take-offs and landings every year?), he walked all the way to the back of the room to sit at the desk next to mine. Right in front of me, Sissie Hornell snickered.

Everyone in Speech 101, Period 5, knew that Harold Brenski had a crush on Maggie Williams. Knowing Sissie's mouth, probably anyone in school who cared about that sort of thing also knew.

Harold really isn't such a bad guy if you like the type of boy who prefers machine mechanics over movies or if you don't mind the smell of grease and oil that has apparently permeated his entire wardrobe.

I was scared to death he'd ask me out. Then what would I do? Turn down my first-ever offer? But I didn't think I was quite desperate enough to accept.

So, as much to get away from Harold as to help compensate for my tardiness, I did a very uncharacteristic thing. When Mrs. Sutherlin asked for the next volunteer, my arm was the first one up.

"OK, Maggie," said Mrs. Sutherlin with a quick smile.

Generally one of the last in the class to give her speech, and then coming forward only when volunteered by Mrs. Sutherlin's grade book, I couldn't help but notice the expressions of surprise on my classmates' faces.

No one in the room could have forgotten my first few unsuccessful attempts to recite aloud a simple little one-minute introductory speech. Of course, I've never forgotten the humiliation of standing tongue-tied before a sea of swarming faces. Neither have I forgotten how understanding Mrs. Sutherlin had been all along. She spent many extra hours helping me devise special tricks to overcome my fright. One technique in particular called controlled breathing seemed to help a lot.

Remembering Mrs. Sutherlin's coaching, I started pacing myself the minute I stood. As I walked the length of the room, I concentrated on my breathing, taking deep, rhythmic breaths, exhaling slowly and fully.

At the front of the class, I straightened my notecards by tapping them upon the podium, another trick Mrs. Sutherlin had taught me to gain a few more seconds' composure time, and looked for Marty Gordon who always sat in the middle section of my "audience." Focusing on Marty keeps me from staring at the ceiling while I'm speaking. The other reason I pick Marty is that by now I knew Marty always cat napped during everyone else's speech. That way, I got to look at a very non-threatening head of brown hair rather than at someone's incriminating stare.

I surprised everyone, most notably myself, by making it through the entire speech without any sudden stops or turning red-faced with embarrassment. I could tell by the way I felt inside and from the look on Mrs. Sutherlin's face that this time I'd made real progress.

The remaining three periods seemed to last forever, but finally school was out for the day.

I dashed over to meet Bren. I wanted to hear more about the opening for a Petite model on Farland's Board, but I was just as anxious to compare notes on the new boy. I'd watched for Matt at every break, but hadn't spotted him again.

As I'd hoped, Bren was already waiting for me.

"How'd your speech go?" she called.

"Great! Better than great. I even volunteered."

That's *good*, Maggie. Now you're in perfect form to go after that position on the Board."

She gave me a conspiratory grin, grabbed her jacket, slammed the locker door with a back kick, and strolled off down the hall without me.

"Hey, Jackson, you rat! I wasn't finished in there yet."

I hurriedly redialed the combination, pulled out my own coat, and ran after her.

"Come on, Bren. Spill!" I commanded, catching up with her. "Tell me exactly how we plan to get me that position. I'll do anything."

"It's quite simple, actually. You fill out an application, you return it to Farland's by Monday, and then you go for your personal interview, at which time you convince Mrs. MacDonald that you're her one and only option."

You mean this is a wide-open competition? Forget it. Do you know how many shorties there are in this school? Carol Conners for one, and she just got that glamorous new perm." Her image rose up before me, fresh in my memory. Obviously the new boy had been impressed with Carol's appearance.

"Don't worry, Maggie, you're a natural."

"I just hope Mrs. MacDonald agrees. How about driving me down to Farland's to pick up an application while I've still got the nerve to go through with it."

Brenda smiled and began rummaging through the papers in her note-book. She pulled out an official-looking form and shoved it at me.

"Here, I saved you the trouble."

Bren *does* come through when it's something vital! In my hands I held

the possibility of a magnificent new me. The more I thought about it, however, the more those hands began to get all sweaty.

"I don't know, Bren. Do you really think I'd be good enough? I'm not as outgoing as you are, you know."

"For Pete's sake, Maggie, you don't have to be an extrovert to be a model. All you have to do is walk around, smile, look friendly, and act confident. It'd be good for you."

Seeing the skeptical look on my face, Bren took a breath and kept on talking, doing her best to convince me I could do it.

"Look, it's easy. First you get picked, that's the only tricky part. Then you'll go through a little course that will teach you all about the right way to walk and turn and so on. Everyone will help you, Maggie. We're always lending each other piles of moral support.

"Besides that, dummy, you get paid," she went on. "With all the money you'll be making and your Farland's discount, you can buy lots of neat new clothes, and then you'll look glamorous all the time . . . just like me."

"Oh, boy, Jackson, you really know how to lay it on thick. I think you're pursuing the wrong profession. Ever consider politics?"

"Not yet," she answered smugly, "but give me some time, who knows?"

As we climbed in Bren's orange Volkswagen, affectionately known as "Betsy," I thought that now would be as good a time as any to bring up Matt.

"By the way, I ran into your new dreamboat on my way to Speech. He's not as tall as you think," I said coyly. "I come up to here on him." I indicated a spot just above my collar bone.

"You wicked little shrimp. Didn't waste a minute, did you? Come on, spill, how'd you manage it?"

Leaving out the part where I became hypnotized just gazing into Matt's fantastic blue eyes, I gave Bren a detailed description of the calamity in the hallway, including Carol's snide reference to me as an "underclassman."

"She could have at least said 'underclasswoman,' " joked Bren.

I asked Bren to come over to my house to help me get the Farland's application filled out.

"I would, but Mom has a four-o'clock class and I promised John I'd take care of Freddy today. Why don't you come over to our place, though? I'll make Freddy play outside so we can concentrate," she offered. John was Bren's older brother, Freddy was her rambunctious five-year-old brother.

I almost said OK—I always enjoy the constant hustle and bustle at the Jackson house—but then I remembered that this was the day that Dad had planned to take Cherub to the veterinarian's office. I wanted to be there when he got home to find out what Dr. Hill thought was wrong with our male puppy.

"How is Cherub?" asked Bren, after I'd explained why I wanted her to take me home. "He hasn't gotten worse, has he?"

"I don't think so, but Dad's been acting awfully worried. I'm not sure he's telling me everything."

Had it really only been four months since Dad and I went out to the kennel to pick out our puppies? They now seemed such permanent members of our household.

We'd gone after one puppy, but came home with two. My line of thinking was that if *I* were a dog, I'd appreciate having a canine companion, someone to whom I could relate.

Dad had laughed at my idea, but he agreed that even though most of his research was conducted in his office right at home, there would be times when he'd have to leave, and yes, with two puppies, there'd be little chance for either dog to feel lonely.

From a litter of eight fat, furry critters, Dad chose the most aggressive and rambunctious of the group and named him Cherub. Right from the start, Cherub was the dominant one. My little Cookie always ended up on the bottom of their wrestling matches, crying uncle with a squeal. Dad and I often joined in. Rolling around on the living-room floor together, we felt like one big happy family, a feeling that was too often missing from our lives since Mom's death.

After Mom's long struggle had ended, Dad and I moved to Alaska as soon as all the legal matters were settled and our house was sold.

He and Mom had already planned the move. For a professor of geological research, Alaska held endless opportunities for firsthand studies of earthquakes, volcanoes, and rock formations. But they'd put it off when Mom's illness became apparent because Dad wanted Mom to have quick access to the best medical treatment available. Not that it had helped.

Everyone agreed that the best medicine for both Dad and me would be to leave behind the faces and places where the painful memories of our happy years with Mom ran deepest, and to do it as quickly as possible.

However I'd seen little sign that Dad's loneliness for Mom had eased any until Cherub and Cookie came along putting new love into our lives.

But lately, Cherub hadn't seemed his usual self. He preferred lying around a lot more than Cookie, who now became the antagonist, always trying to tease and provoke him into another wrestling match.

What really broke my heart was to watch Cherub as he tried to obey Dad's command to "load up" into the back of our Bronco. Cookie had no problem. With one leap, she was inside and jumping around. But each time Cherub tried to jump up, his front feet just managed to claw at the edge of the tailgate while his rear paws scrambled to make contact with the bumper.

Finally he'd fall down to the ground, but not before his chin had banged sharply against the metal tailgate. Cherub, innately stubborn, would try over and over again to obey Dad's command, until Dad would go over and pick up his puppy and gently put him inside with Cookie.

"What's wrong with him, Dad?" I'd asked.

"Well, honey, I'm not too sure. But it seems to me that Cherub's muscles aren't as developed as Cookie's. He just can't seem to push himself off the ground like she can."

He ran his fingers through his hair, a habit of nervousness Dad's had for as long as I can remember, and added, "If his condition doesn't improve soon, I'm going to have to take him in to see Dr. Hill."

It hadn't. In fact, I thought I could see Cookie getting bigger and stronger every day, while Cherub, although he weighed more than she did, got weaker.

"It's not his muscles, Maggie, it's in his hip joint," Dad told me when I got home. "Dr. Hill called it hip dysplasia."

"Can he cure it? Will it stop. . .or get worse?"

"Well, the doctor isn't certain at this point. He gave me some medicine for Cherub. One kind for pain and another that may reduce the effects of the disease, but other than painful and not always successful surgery, right now veterinary medicine has no real cure for the disease."

"But how did he get it? Can Cookie catch it from him?"

"No. It's an inherited disease, according to Dr. Hill, and not all that uncommon in golden retrievers. It is unusual for it to show up in a dog as young as Cherub, but Dr. Hill thinks Cherub's husky build may have brought on the symptoms a little sooner."

I could tell by my Dad's face that he was really worried. I knew he was trying to sound optimistic and brave for my benefit, so I went with my instincts and reached out and gave him a great, big hug.

It seemed to help, because when I stepped back from him, there was a smile on his face and he whispered, "Thanks, honey."

I mumbled some excuse about doing my homework and headed for the stairway to my room.

Mostly I needed to get away from Cherub because right then, just looking at his innocent, unknowing little face made me want to start crying.

Without thinking about it, I ran up the stairs so fast that both dogs thought I was playing. I turned around at the sound of some noisy thumping in time to see Cherub tumbling back down the stairs.

Cookie had come bounding after me and naturally Cherub had tried to keep up with her. He only cried out with one little squeal, picked himself back up, and made ready to attempt the steep stairway again. But Dad had already come to the rescue, grabbing Cherub up in his arms, saying, "OK, little fella, enough mountaineering for one day. Time you and your sister went outside for a while."

I gave Cookie some affection, then ordered her back down the stairs where Dad was getting ready to take her and Cherub out for a walk.

Before I made it all the way into my room though, I thought of another question and so I called back down the stairway:

"Dad, how long did Dr. Hill say it would be until that pain medicine started working?"

"We should notice some improvement this week, Maggie."

I didn't like the way his voice emphasized the word *should*.

Alone in my room, I forced myself to open the notebook in front of me. Glaring back at me was the Fashion Board application. With all my concern about Cherub, I'd completely forgotten to tell Dad about my chance to become a model.

I considered running after him to share the news, but I got sidetracked looking over the application form. I decided to begin filling it out right away.

The form began with a series of pretty basic questions: name, date of birth, school subjects, grades, hobbies, and special interests. Then there were five blank lines upon which I was to enter the reasons why I wanted to become a Board member. I skipped that part, deciding to give Bren a call in a little while for her ideas on what to say.

Then I came to the bottom of the page where a parent and a school counselor had to sign. That's when I saw the words that instantly threw me into a horrible state of despair.

"Sponsor swears that applicant is presently 16 years of age or older."

I was still only 15!

3

I phoned Bren immediately, hoping, praying, for a ready-made solution to the situation. After all, getting my hopes up about becoming a Farland's model was her doing. Surely she'd known about the age requirement.

"Bren, I won't turn 16 until the 22nd. That's more than two weeks away and you said the applications are due this Monday!"

"Oh, Maggie, I'm sorry. I always forget we aren't the same age."

My only reply was a loud sigh of exasperation. How could she have forgotten something as basic as my 16th birthday?

"Now, don't panic. I know Mrs. MacDonald. She's very fair. The fact that your birthday misses the deadline by a few days . . ."

"By more than two weeks!" I corrected.

"OK, by a couple of weeks. I still think if you simply explain the situation and tell her how much the chance to apply means to you, I bet she'd say OK."

"Well, I guess that's what I'll *have* to do," I said, resigning myself to the fact that there really were no other options, besides giving up. I may be a klutz at talking sometimes, but I'm certainly no quitter.

"That's the spirit! Tomorrow morning just as soon as the store opens, call her up and ask for an appointment."

"Don't you think I could just ask her about it over the phone?"

"No, Maggie. I think she'd be more sympathetic meeting you face-to-face."

Even though I eventually agreed to Bren's plan of approach, the uncertainty of the situation left me feeling a little depressed, which made me think of Cherub.

I considered telling Bren about Dr. Hill's diagnosis, but decided to wait a while. For some reason I haven't quite figured out, just saying something aloud often seems to make it more real.

As soon as we'd settled on the plan with Mrs. MacDonald, Bren brought up a more cheerful subject.

"Hey, I really didn't forget you had a birthday coming up. What are we going to do to celebrate? You must have thought about it, Maggie. We'll throw a party, of course—remember how great mine was last year?"

She was right. Bren's 16th birthday party had been fantastic. It was the weekend just before Halloween. Bren's older brother, John, and some of his senior-class friends turned the Jackson place into the scariest haunted house trip I've ever had the opportunity to scream my way through. The spooky course ended in the Jacksons' huge recreation room where rock-and-roll music filled the air. A large area had been cleared of furniture to create a dance floor.

Word spread fast. I'll bet half of Ridgeway High showed up before the night was over.

Unfortunately, midway throught the evening, I found myself at the center of the single disheartening event of the entire evening. We were all sitting around pigging out on birthday cake and ice cream when someone wondered aloud if perhaps it would be appropriate for Brenda's best friend to present the birthday toast.

Everyone quickly agreed. The music stopped and hush fell over the entire room. And there stood Maggie, a glass of punch raised in the air, an appropriate toast in her mind, and a tongue that wouldn't cooperate with its owner.

As usual, Bren had come to my rescue, commenting cutely that she hadn't realized there wasn't a single nice thing her friend could say about her.

"So, what do you say, birthday girl—want to have your party at my house?" Bren asked, bringing my thoughts back to the present.

"Could we? Your mom wouldn't mind?"

Using their five-bedroom home instead of our two-bedroom town house would certainly make compiling a guest list a lot easier. There would be plenty of room for all our friends at Bren's place.

"Would my mother mind if we throw your one and only 16th birthday party in her house? You know better than that, Maggie Williams," she reprimanded. It was true that Mrs. Jackson treated me like a second daughter.

We spend the next 20 minutes brainstorming on party ideas. I was just getting ready to lead the conversation around to Matt, maybe to hint at how I couldn't seem to get him off my mind, when Dad hollered at me to say good-night.

I slept terribly that night, dreaming of an ogrelike Mrs. MacDonald who refused to consider any sort of exception to the rules. Bending over a miniature Maggie, Mrs. MacDonald appeared to be at least eight feet tall. By the way she shook her finger in my face, I could tell that she abhorred the idea of allowing short girls to model in the first place.

Maybe nightmares are helpful in a roundabout way because the next day when I called Farland's and asked for Mrs. MacDonald, I was prepared for the worst. Instead a friendly, cheery voice came on the line.

"This is Mrs. MacDonald. May I help you?"

Unfortunately, even though we weren't speaking face-to-face, I'd worked up so much anxiety over the impending conversation that once again I was overcome with speechlessness.

Suddenly all I could think of was: *She doesn't yet know who's on the line, she can't say no if she doesn't know to whom she's talking.*

The absurdity of this reasoning finally broke through when I heard her getting ready to hang up.

"Hello. Is anyone there?" she asked, her increasing irritation evident by the tone of her voice.

"Yes! This is Maggie Williams. I'm sorry, there must be something wrong with this phone," I added. "I couldn't hear you."

"That's OK. How can I help you, Maggie?" She sounded nice again, so I relaxed a little.

"Brenda Jackson told me about your new opening for a petite model. I'd like to apply. I even have the application nearly completed. But there's one requirement I'd like the opportunity to come in and talk with you about."

"Oh? Why don't we just discuss it right now? If you are a friend of Brenda's, I'm certain you're a sweet girl whom we'd be happy to have on our Board, providing of course you meet all our basic requirements."

"That's the problem. I'm two weeks away from my 16th birthday," I blurted out, relieved that she'd rejected the in-person approach.

"I see," was her only reply.

Oh-oh. Maybe Bren had been right. Perhaps I'd just blown my chances. Suddenly scared that the impersonal nature of the telephone would allow Mrs. MacDonald to dismiss me and my problem more easily, I plunged right ahead.

"I mean, you really wouldn't be suspending any regulations, only postponing them for a couple of weeks. Oh, Mrs. MacDonald, I just know I'd make a great model for Farland's. It'd be a dream come true for me. Please, would you consider allowing me to apply?"

I thought of how disappointed Mrs. Sutherlin would have been if she could have overheard my poorly organized presentation. Even so, I could almost hear Mrs. MacDonald thinking over my situation.

At last she said, "Hold the line just a minute, Maggie, would you please? Let me take a look at Monday's schedule."

She was going to say OK! I concentrated on my controlled breathing until I heard her pick up the receiver again.

"Can you bring your application in on Monday, right after school?"

"I can be there by 3:30."

"Fine, Maggie. I'll see you then for a preliminary interview. Then we'll discuss your predicament with the age requirement, OK?"

"Oh, thank you, Mrs. MacDonald! See you Monday!"

I knew my voice sounded breathless—I felt like shouting "Hurray!" out loud. She hadn't said I couldn't apply and she was actually going to interview me. My impression of Mrs. MacDonald was that she *was* the understanding sort, after all.

I'd find out soon enough. Monday was only four days away.

At lunch, Brenda was ready with the latest gossip from the junior class grapevine but insisted I go first with the news of my morning call.

"Well? What'd she say?"

"She asked me to bring my application and come in for a preliminary interview Monday after school. She said we'd discuss my situation then. So what do you think? I'm not in, but at least I'm not out."

"Sounds highly promising, is what I think. More promising than anyone's chances at turning Matt Brennan's head now that Carol Conners has glomped onto him."

"What?" I blurted, her words confirming my unspoken fears.

"Well," said Bren, swinging her long legs up onto the empty lunch table bench across from her, "true to the Conners reputation, she's already asked Matt Brennan to go to the Spring Dance with her. Word is that she gave him the welcome-wagon treatment last night at the Super Duper. I can just picture her: 'Oh, Matt, it must be so hard to be the new kid in school. Let me be your friend.' "

The Super Duper is our local fast-food hangout. Bren's imitation of Carol wasn't half-bad. I probably would have been laughing a lot harder if it hadn't been for the disappointment I felt.

The Spring Dance was only a couple of weeks away. I'd planned on attending since you didn't *have* to come with a date, and had already entertained daydreams of getting to know Matt Brennan a little better at the dance.

"According to Sissie, who says this is all straight from Carol, Ms.

Upperclasswoman herself," Bren broke off in laughter; my spirits dampened but I pretended to join in. ". . . Matt is a pilot. His uncle has an airplane out on Lake Hood and he told Carol he's been flying it every chance he gets ever since he got here."

"So now Carol has decided to add a pilot to her collection," I reflected, hoping the sarcasm in my voice would cover up the bitterness I felt toward Carol.

"Apparently so," answered Bren. "They're both in my Trig class. I don't think Matt noticed anything Mr. Garland wrote on the blackboard this morning; he was too busy studying Ms. Well-Proportioned herself."

I felt relieved that I hadn't had time to bring up the subject of Matt on the phone the previous evening. Now that Carol had her claws into him, it was better that no one knew about my fledgling crush on Matt Brennan, not even Bren.

Over the weekend, Bren and I fine-tuned the personal statement on my application, then role-played the upcoming interview, with Bren trying to remember the kinds of questions Mrs. MacDonald had asked her.

Then Bren checked her work calendar and discovered that she'd promised one of the other girls on the Board to work for her that weekend, so we moved my party up another week. I began to get the feeling that fate was working against my ever reaching my 16th birthday.

I spent the rest of my weekend with Dad and the puppies. We went down to the beach by the inlet to run and play with Cherub and Cookie. Cherub's hips seemed to be doing pretty well. Neither Dad nor I mentioned it, but I could tell that we were both feeling hopeful that the pills Dad quietly fed Cherub three times a day would gradually eliminate his problems.

Monday flew by in a panic as I tried to chase down my counselor, Mr. Knoll, from classroom to classroom. Three times, I'd just missed him. His signature on my application was the only incomplete item.

At last I caught up with him on my free period, over in the shop building. When I walked into the auto-mechanics room, there he stood talking to none other than Matt Brennan, who held a large socket wrench in his hands, turning it end over end, a little impatiently, I thought, while he shook his head at whatever Mr. Knoll was saying to him.

"Oh, Maggie," Mr. Knoll said when he saw me, "I was headed over to study hall to find you just as soon as I finished checking in with our new student here. Have you met Matt yet?"

I wasn't certain that Matt would remember me so I didn't know what to say. Luckily, Mr. Knoll, in his usual manner, didn't give me a chance to reply either way. He continued right on into an introduction.

To my surprise, Matt interrupted Mr. Knoll, saying, "Maggie and I've already had the pleasure of an introduction. In fact, we bumped into each other on my first day, before I knew which way was up around here."

Matt looked me straight in the eyes as he spoke to Mr. Knoll. When he finished, I was so elated that he not only remembered me—of course, who could forget an incident like that on his first day at a new school—but also that he remembered my name, which at the time made me as happy as if he'd just asked me for a date.

Naturally, I couldn't think of a reply quickly enough, so I just smiled at him shyly and handed Mr. Knoll my application.

Instead of simply signing the paper, Mr. Knoll had to make it into a big production. He sat down and began to read the whole thing carefully from top to bottom, while Matt and I stood waiting in an uncomfortable silence.

Now's your chance to talk to him, I told myself. Bren said he's from your hometown, ask him about Portland; maybe you have some mutual acquaintances.

Before I got my courage up though—who knows how long that would have taken—Matt said, "So you're a model?"

"Well, not yet," I answered, thinking he sounded impressed by the idea.

"I thought models were tall," commented Matt.

That's when I realized I'd misinterpreted the surprised tone in his voice tone in his voice for admiration and awe. Actually it had been amazement that anyone as low to the ground as myself would consider herself modeling material.

So my voice may have sounded a bit on the defensive side when I answered, "Not if they're modeling clothing for girls under 5′2″."

It looked as though this conversation with Matt weren't going to last much longer than the first one. I checked on Mr. Knoll. Why wasn't he finished yet?

When I saw Mr. Knoll frown as he looked at the bottom of the page, I realized I was in for some more embarrassment in front of Matt.

"Maggie, this says I'm supposed to verify that you're 16. From the information you've supplied here, your birthday is still a couple of weeks away."

"I know, Mr. Knoll, and I've already discussed it with the Board supervisor. I still need your signature."

"Well, I'll have to amend this verification segment. Sorry."

He made it sound as though I was trying to slip something in on him, to cheat! I wanted to defend myself, but I knew that any after-the-fact attempt to explain my situation would only sound as if I were trying to cover up.

Matt discreetly wandered off to the other side of the shop and began tinkering with a disassembled motor. I waited impatiently for Mr. Knoll's signature above the amendment that he was carefully penning in: "Sponsor attests that applicant will turn 16 years of age on the 22nd of March."

As soon as he finished, I snatched the application from his hand and headed for the nearest door, seeking the fastest possible retreat from the shop building's unfamiliar and hostile environment.

Unfortunately, there was no escape from the memory of how foolish and childish I must have appeared in Matt's eyes.

4

Seated in the waiting room outside Mrs. MacDonald's office later that afternoon, my love life, or rather the lack of one, was the last thing on my mind.

I'd expected to walk into a room lined with wall-to-wall applicants. Instead, there was only myself and Mrs. MacDonald's receptionist—a skinny, somewhat homely woman with large teeth and bushy hair. A sign on her desk read "Ms. Grimley." I gave the woman my name and the time for which my appointment was scheduled.

Ms. Grimley pushed a buzzer, asked me to take a seat, and without another word, turned her attention back to the magazine that lay open across her desk. With nothing else to do but wait, I chose a fashion magazine from the stack beside me and stared at incomprehensible words upon the pages.

After an unbearably slow five minutes had passed, the box on Ms. Grimley's desk began to emit an annoying beeping sound. Ms. Grimley pushed another button on the box, then she answered Mrs. MacDonald's call with a sugary-sweet voice.

"Yes, Mrs. MacDonald."

"Please ask Maggie to come in now, Ms. Grimley."

As I made my way toward the large oak-paneled door that Ms. Grimley had motioned for me to enter, my knees were shaking visibly and I felt as though they would give out before I could make it across the room.

I knocked lightly at the door and Mrs. MacDonald called out for me to enter.

The first thing that struck me as I entered Mrs. MacDonald's office was the contrast between the outer waiting area, and this inner, private office. Although it was much larger than the small reception area, that wasn't what I noticed as much as the furnishings it contained. Primarily contemporary in style with touches of nostalgia, the total effect was that of a private, cozy sitting room. I felt myself relax by a degree or two.

"So you're Maggie Williams," said a pleasant-looking woman, who was certainly not the ogre from my dream. "It's nice to meet you, but don't think that your distressful phone call was the first time I'd heard your name. You have a very good friend in Brenda Jackson. She's often spoken highly of you."

Mrs. MacDonald's warm, relaxed greeting evoked such a strong sense of familiarity between us that for a minute I forgot I was about to receive the most important, not to mention the only, interview of my life.

"Thank you. I've heard a lot about you too," I told her.

She laughed in a light, easy way that insinuated she could imagine the kinds of things I'd heard. "All good, of course," I added quickly.

"Of course," she answered with a smile.

"I love your office. It's beautiful."

"Thank you. I spend so much time here, it's really my home away from home. Well, Maggie, shall we get started?"

She led me away from the area of her large, cluttered desk to the far corner of the room. Two comfortable-looking love seats, divided by a small coffee table, faced each other. But what captured my attention was the immense picture window that provided the room with a sixth-floor view of Mount McKinley. The day was clear and we had a perfect sight of North America's tallest mountain.

We admired the spectacular mountain for a moment, then Mrs. MacDonald jumped right into the business at hand.

"Maggie, we included the age requirement because state law requires that our models be at least 16 years of age to work at any job after 9 P.M., which is sometimes the case when we work an evening show."

I listened attentively, trying my best to hide the feelings of disappointment I felt stirring as I realized she was trying to tell me in a nice, but roundabout, way that I would not qualify.

"I'll be conducting interviews all week," she continued, "selecting candidates for the final interviewing session next Saturday. It'll take at least another week before the new Board member will be show-ready—she'll have to work hard to catch up with the other girls—and by that time, should you be the lucky one, you will have already celebrated your 16 birthday, and voila!, no more problem. OK?"

I could hardly believe my ears. "That's wonderful news, Mrs. Mac-Donald. Thank you!"

"Well, you may want to save your thanks for later. I haven't begun the interview yet."

An authoritative tone in her voice told me that she *did* know how to give orders and that she *would* expect them to be carried out in a conscientious manner.

For the next hour, Mrs. MacDonald questioned me on everything from my family and friends, to school studies, to my plans for the future. She didn't seem to mind that, unlike many of my friends, I really hadn't yet formed any set career goals. She told me I still had plenty of time and that most people change their minds along the way anyhow.

"I notice you're enrolled in Speech 101. That's very smart, Maggie. Oratory skills are a valuable tool in almost any line of endeavor."

Oh, boy, I thought to myself, *if she only knew the real reason I'd enrolled, and how much suffering I'd gone through to maintain a respectable grade in that class*. I smiled, nodded my head, and kept my mouth shut, not bothering to mention my "problem."

When Mrs. MacDonald had finally exhausted her seemingly endless list of questions, she thanked me for coming and told me I'd hear from her by Friday if she wanted me back for the final interviews on Saturday.

The intensity with which I'd concentrated on giving intelligent and personable replies during the interview had zapped me. As I headed for my bike, I felt a lightheaded disorientation, as though the last hour had not been real.

But real it had been. As I imagined what it would be like actually to get up on stage in front of a crowd of people, a thrill of excitement tingled through me. Sure I wondered where I'd find the nerve, but at the same time, more than anything, I desperately wanted the opportunity to prove to myself I could do it.

Not much else happened the rest of the week. All I wanted was for Friday to come and go so that the anxiety of not knowing about the Fashion Board position would pass.

I saw Matt in the hallways a few times but Carol was always with him. I wondered why he let her hang around him so much; she seemed so different from Matt. Of course, deep down I *knew* why: for the same reasons any other boy at Ridgeway High would have dropped anything for a chance with Carol. She knew how to flirt and tease and make a boy feel special in her presence. All I knew was that I was no competition for Carol.

Cherub had been moving around like an old dog ever since our outing on Sunday. Watching him just got me more depressed so I was really a nervous wreck by the time Friday finally arrived.

Although Mrs. MacDonald hadn't indicated exactly how or when on Friday the finalists would be notified, I'd expected her to call us at home after school. So when an office messenger brought a note to my Social Studies teacher that requested I report to Mr. Knoll's office at the break, I had the awful premonition that it would be bad news about Cherub.

I saw Bren during the break but was in such a hurry to find out about my message that I merely waved and rushed on by.

As I approached Mr. Knoll's office, I remembered my *last* meeting with him, over in the shop building. That's when I realized that he just might be waiting with word from Mrs. MacDonald. She'd promised to make sure that each girl was notified, one way or the other, so that no one would wait up all night deluding herself needlessly.

When I entered Mr. Knoll's office, he said, "Ah! If it isn't my petite little model."

Did he know something I didn't? Or was he just being his usual facetious self? I strained against my desire to give him a dirty look. When I didn't reply, he continued: "I have a message from Mrs. MacDonald requesting that you call her at your earliest convenience. You may use my phone if you like."

It suddenly struck me that Mr. Knoll would like nothing better than for me to use his phone so that he could conveniently listen in on my important call. So, no matter that I was dying to make that call, I thanked him politely and excused myself, heading for the pay phones down the hall.

I ignored the ringing of the tardy bell—it seemed I was destined to rack up more tardies this semester than I'd ever had in all my years of school—and made ready to jog down the deserted hallway. Just then Mrs. Sutherlin came around the corner.

My first instinct was to dodge her. I didn't have the time to explain what I was doing in the halls during class time. But she'd already spotted me and so I knew that my phone call would be delayed further.

"Maggie! What are you doing on this end of campus? Don't you have Mr. Glasier's class this hour?"

"Yes, Mrs. Sutherlin, but I got called to Mr. Knoll's office for a message. I've got to return an important call."

"My office is right here," she said understandingly. "Why don't you go on inside and make your call? I'll be back shortly. I wanted to go to the teachers' room for coffee and the latest gossip before I settled down to some paper grading, anyway."

Amazed by her perceptivity, I thanked her gratefully and strode purposefully into her office to make my call.

I dialed Farland's number, asked for Mrs. MacDonald's extension, and got the sugar-sweet receptionist on the line. When I told her it was Maggie Williams calling, she turned on her super syrupy voice. Of course, this only served to heighten my level of anxiety. Was she just trying to be nice? To soften the blow?

"Mrs. MacDonald is on another line right now, Maggie. But I know she's anxious to speak with you. Can you please hold for a moment?"

I waited for a minute that took forever, then Mrs. MacDonald came on the line.

"Maggie! Can you come in tomorrow at one o'clock for another interview?"

Do cows eat grass?

"Yes, Mrs. MacDonald. Thank you! See you tomorrow."

I was still in the running, a finalist! For the very first time, I began to let myself believe I might just make it all the way.

I don't know how long I'd been sitting in Mrs. Sutherlin's chair with my feet propped up on her desk when she knocked gently and entered the room with a cup of steaming coffee in her hands.

I jumped up from her chair, my mouth working on the beginnings of a lengthy apology, but she nonchalantly motioned for me to sit back down while she took a seat in the less comfortable wooden chair beside me.

"From the look on your face, I'd say the call brought good news."

"I'll say!" I nearly exploded, I was so anxious to share my wonderful news with another living being. "I'm a finalist for Farland's new Fashion Board position."

"Congratulations, Maggie. What's next?"

"I go in for a final interview tomorrow." Then reality hit me. "I wonder how may other finalists there are?"

"Well, I wouldn't tell just anyone, but I did see Carol Conners and Sheila Hayes come and go last hour with faces lit up just like yours. I also saw some other girls who apparently didn't fare so well."

Carol again! I should have known she'd apply. Well, that finished it.

She was a sure winner. She already walked and talked and dressed as I imagined a model should.

Mrs. Sutherlin must have read my face because then she said, "Hey, the interview isn't until tomorrow. The position is still anybody's. You remember that, Maggie."

Then she artfully changed the topic of conversation to the upcoming Spring Dance. She told me she was in charge of arranging for the chaperones and that so far she had enough teachers to help out, but she still needed additional parent volunteers.

"Do you think your folks might be willing to give up a Saturday night?" she asked.

A cloud passed over my face at her mention of my "folks." I was thinking of how if my mother were still alive she'd volunteer in a minute. Unlike Dad, she'd always been extremely social and outgoing, always in the middle of any plans for special occasions.

"Oh, Maggie, I'm so sorry. How thoughtless of me to forget."

Of course, Mrs. Sutherlin would have been informed of my mother's death at the beginning of the semester, as that event was presumably at the root of my speech handicap. The subject probably had been discussed extensively by Mr. Knoll when he'd enrolled me in her class.

"No, please don't feel bad, Mrs. Sutherlin. It doesn't bother me to talk about her any more, not like it used to, anyway."

"You know, Maggie, I was very proud of you last week. You not only volunteered to give your speech, you gave it without a hitch. I suspect what you just told me about feeling more comfortable about your mother's death may have something to do with your progress."

I hadn't thought about it that way, but the minute she suggested it, I knew it was true. However I still didn't consider myself entirely cured of the problem. I doubted that she had any idea how nervous I still felt anytime I stood up to speak.

We visited a while longer, despite the fact that I was missing most of Mr. Glasier's algebra class. In class, Mrs. Sutherlin had always seemed excessively formal and aloof. On the other hand, I'd always found her easy to talk to on a one-to-one basis. I suppose she thought that during class time she had to uphold the image of a "proper" instructor. As I considered the apparent discrepancy in Mrs. Sutherlin's personality, I realized that my mother, whom I'd always considered to be the epitome of warmth and kindness, had probably come across to her students much the same as Mrs. Sutherlin.

By the time Mrs. Sutherlin gave me a late pass to get into Mr. Glasier's class, the period was nearly over. Then there was only art and study hall to get through before I could meet Bren at our locker to tell her the good news.

On my way to study hall, Carol and a bunch of her friends came toward me, talking excitedly. I supposed she was sharing her news about making it as a Fashion Board finalist.

But as Carol and the others passed by, I distinctly caught the sounds of two words: Matt Brennan. And then, something about the Spring Dance.

So it was true. Some girls have all the luck. Not only would Carol be the likely choice for the Fashion Board, she'd won the heart of the neatest boy in school, as well.

What? Was I really thinking those thoughts? I gave myself a mental reprimand. I had no business feeling jealous of Carol over Matt. Even if he had remembered me from our accidental run-in, I knew from past experience that any interest he might have in me would be strictly on a good-friend basis.

Besides, I wasn't ready for boyfriends. It was painfully obvious that I hadn't an inkling of how to get one or how to act around one. Bren kept telling me it would all come naturally when the right time and guy came along. But like the celebration of my 16th birthday, I was beginning to wonder if the right time or boy would ever arrive.

5

I got to our locker just as Bren arrived.

"Well, I talked to Mrs. MacDonald. I'm a finalist!"

"Maggie, congratulations! That's great news. So how come you look like you *didn't* make it?"

"Probably because Carol also made it to the finals. I already know she'll win out over me." *Just like she's already won Matt,* I thought to myself.

"I wouldn't be so sure about that. Models aren't supposed to be so. . . ." Bren formed large cups with her hands in front of her chest.

We both laughed, then I added, "Yes, but I'll bet she could sell a lot of bathing suits!"

At home that night, I got the feeling that Dad was as surprised as I that I'd actually made the finals. At first, he was less than enthusiastic. Naturally his primary concern was that my grades would slip.

"You're sure it won't take too much time away from your studies? You've got to consider what's ahead of you, Maggie."

"Oh, Dad, don't be such a spoilsport. I'm finally attempting to add a social, more outgoing element to my personality. I thought that's what you and Mr. Knoll were encouraging me to do."

"You're right, honey," he conceded. "Something like this is exactly what you need. Truth is, I'm probably just jealous, because if you win, it'll take away from the time you spend with me."

"Oh, Dad. It won't take *all* my time. And if I *do* get the position, I'll also have a part-time job at the store." The idea of earning money of my own was almost as exciting and important to me as the opportunity to model.

"OK, but before you become so overwhelmingly in demand, how about putting Cherub, Cookie, and me on your schedule for a trip to Portage Glacier this Sunday?"

Both puppies overheard their names and came running from the other room to entangle themselves between our legs, competing for attention and affection. As I reached down to pet them, the truth of Dad's words hit home.

If, by some wild miscalculation, I should happen to end up on the Board, my absences from home would indeed become frequent. I felt a sudden ambivalence about winning. I'm certain Dad detected the sentiment in my voice when I finally answered.

"Of course I'll go, Dad. But really, you don't have to worry about it. My chances of winning are pretty slim."

"What do you mean, Maggie?"

"Well, there's some stiff competition, especially from this one girl, Carol Conners."

"There's always going to be stiff competition in whatever endeavor you pursue in this world, young lady. Just so you give it your best."

As there really wasn't anything to be said in reply to his words of wisdom, I just gave him my best loving-daughter smile in thanks for his concern.

Then I let myself fall to the living-room carpet, an open invitation for an attack from Cherub and Cookie. I glanced back up at Dad. He was staring off into space, as if he were trying to figure something out.

At last he said, "Maggie, I hope my concentration on your academic endeavors hasn't damaged your social development. It's just that I've never been as socially adept as your mother. I miss her suggestions and guidance in raising you." He paused a minute. I didn't know how to answer him, as I was afraid he was right.

"However it turns out, I want you to know that I'm very proud and supportive of the initiative you've taken pursuing this goal."

"Thanks, Dad," I said, wishing he knew how to talk to me without sounding like a professor all the time.

"And I haven't finished reserving time on your social calendar yet. I've heard you talking about attending some school dance that's on the night of your birthday, so I want us to celebrate with a fancy dinner the night before. Agreed?"

"Agreed."

I got up from the floor and gave Dad a hug. The puppies followed my example, committing the ultimate sin of climbing up onto the couch. They got away with it, though, by giving Dad some slobbery puppy kisses.

Later that evening, Bren called me from Farland's during her break. She told me rumor had it that there were six finalists coming in the next day.

"It really doesn't matter who the others are," I told Bren. "Carol's going to get it."

"Will you knock it off? If you don't start thinking positively, you might as well not even show up tomorrow."

I knew Bren was right.

"OK, not another negative word from my mouth, I promise."

"That's better. Well, I'd better get back to work. Want me to drive you to Farland's tomorrow?"

I gladly accepted her offer. I knew I'd be grateful for the moral support.

"What outfit are you going to wear, anyway? I could come by early and give it my stamp of approval," she offered.

"That'd be great. I don't know what to wear. I planned to work on that tonight."

And that's what I did for the rest of the evening. But nothing in my closet satisfied me, no matter how many new combinations I tried. So I decided to sleep on it since I'd have all morning to put something together.

Thank goodness Bren kept her promise and arrived an hour early or I might still be deciding what I should wear to the interview. When she got there, my entire wordrobe was piled up on my bed. I'd spent three hours wondering which outfit would do the most to make me look like a potential model.

"How about your lavender cotton-knit dress? It's got nice lines that show off your slim figure."

"But I don't have any shoes to match. There's only the brown or the black ones. That dress really needs something softer."

"OK, how about your navy-blue slacks and that fleecy white sweater I like so much. You could add a neck scarf for color."

"The sweater's too tight. Dad did the laundry and put it in the drier. Besides don't you think a dress or skirt would be more appropriate than pants?"

"You're probably right. OK, I've got it," she said, as she rummaged through the pile of clothing. "Take this beige velveteen vest and button it over this silky-looking cream blouse, along with your brown linen skirt. Your brown heels will go perfectly."

"That'd work, I guess. But don't you think the skirt will wrinkle too easily?"

"Don't worry about it. Real linen is supposed to wrinkle. This outfit will show Mrs. MacDonald you've got a good sense of style."

I decided to trust Bren's judgment. Besides, I was running out of time. I tried on the whole outfit, just to make sure, and then took everything off again to iron it all.

My brown hair is thick and long, probably my best asset. I usually wear it straight, with the sides pulled back into a barrette at the back of my head. But Brenda fixed it into a single French braid and then draped it across my shoulder. The look was stylish but well-groomed and even I was pleased with the effect.

I applied my usual scant make-up—some powder blush, a light coat of mascara, and pink-tinted lip gloss—and got into my freshly pressed outfit.

Now that all the choices had been made, as I checked my final appearance in the full-length mirror, a feeling of calmness began to envelop me—a confidence of purpose, a knowledge that whatever will be, will be. Incredibly, I felt that even if I lost, the outcome I considered most likely, I'd be able to handle the rejection without freaking out.

Riding with Brenda down the familiar streets of my adopted home-town, I reminded myself that the experience itself would strengthen my character and, in the long run, that was sufficient reason for enduring the emotional trauma I'd racked upon myself all week.

Surprisingly enough, that new sense of calmness stayed with me all through my 20-minute wait in Mrs. MacDonald's reception room, even when none other than Carol herself came strutting out of Mrs. Mac-Donald's office, looking her usual crisp and cool self.

That's Carol and I'm Maggie, I reminded myself as I tried to smooth the developing wrinkles in my skirt.

The interview went much more quickly than the first one. I got the distinct impression that Mrs. MacDonald had already made her deci-sion, that she was just checking to see that she'd made the right choice by looking us over one more time.

As I was leaving her office, Mrs. MacDonald told me she only had two more girls to interview. She said if I'd come back in an hour, she'd have made her decision by then.

I found Bren looking at clothes in the Junior Department. We decided to kill some time in Cosmetics. Another Board member, Sheri Anderson, was on duty in that department. She wasn't busy with customers, so Bren convinced me to let Sheri do a make-over on me, something Bren had been trying to get me to try for a long time.

As if it were a painter's canvas, Sheri concentrated intently on the col-oring and contouring of my face, but she wouldn't let me watch. Finally satisfied, she held up a mirror to let me see the finished product.

As I looked at my reflection, I was overcome with a feeling of déjà vu, of having seen just such a transformation before. Only it never had been I who was transformed but one of the many girls I'd viewed in *Seventeen* or *Mademoiselle* who'd been lucky enough to receive a professional make-over. The girl who stared back at me in disbelief *looked* like a teen model *should* look. Even Bren seemed impressed.

"Maggie, you look great. We'll take one each of whatever you've used on her," she told Sheri. "Be sure to give Maggie one of those diagrams so she can practice duplicating the procedure."

Sheri handed me a piece of paper with half of a woman's face on it. She'd applied my make-up scheme onto the diagram indicating the order of application.

"Now, don't get frustrated if it doesn't come out just right the first time you try it, Maggie. The trick is to keep everything light and *blend*, so you look natural, not made-up. But it'll take some practice," she cautioned me.

While Sheri bagged my new collection of goodies, I checked the clock above the escalator and saw that it had already been over an hour since I'd left Mrs. MacDonald's office.

"Thanks, Sheri," I said, not really so thankful when I saw the bill she was ringing up. Bren saw my mortified look and told Sheri, "How about putting that on my account, Sheri? You can pay me back later," she assured me when I started to protest. "Come on, let's go get the good news," she added, grabbing my bag of cosmetics and steering me toward the escalator.

When Bren and I walked into the reception area, it was a surprise, and not exactly a pleasant one, to find that Carol was there, too, seated in the chair closest to Mrs. MacDonald's office door. The expression on Carol's face told me that the surprise was mutual. Otherwise the room was empty, even Ms. Grimley was absent.

"Well, Carol, any news from behind the big door yet?" asked Bren, breaking the uncomfortable silence.

"No, not yet, but Mrs. MacDonald asked me to come back at three o'clock, and it's ten after, so I'm just sure she'll be out any minute." She glanced at me suspiciously, then turned back to Bren. "What are *you* doing up here anyway?"

"Oh, just along for the ride. I came in with Maggie to lend some moral support."

"Oh," was all Carol had to say, in a tone that insinuated I'd need it.

Despite the fact that I despised her milk-and-honey complexion, I loved to look at Carol. Her skin was always so perfect, sometimes I wondered if she weren't an android, deftly slipped into Ridgeway High by government agents, to provide an example for all us imperfect human females. And this was my prime competition!

"Mrs. MacDonald asked me to come back too," I informed her nonchalantly. I don't think Carol was very impressed though, because she stared at me briefly, then faced Bren again.

"How do you like being on the Board, Bren?" she asked.

"Well, it's more time-consuming that you might imagine, but the fringe benefits are great. We get discounts on all our purchases, and wages from modeling and from working at the store. We also get free passes to any special event sponsored by Farland's, as long as we wear our special Farland's outfit. I always feel kind of silly wearing the same outfit as nine other girls, but that's part of the arrangement."

Personally, I thought the outfits were great. I don't care what Ann Landers says about personality, boys notice girls with nice clothes.

And I had to admit it, lately I'd become anxious for change, a change in myself. Someone more glamorous, more sophisticated. Someone who attracted attractive boys. Boys like Matt Brennan. Just thinking of what it would be like to walk along on the arm of Matt made me feel queasy inside.

Carol must have been thinking along the same lines, because then she said, "I'll bet you get a lot of guys who ask you out just because you're a model."

Bren laughed. "Not really. But I do get the opportunity to meet guys who play in bands. Lots of times we do our modeling shows in between sets at teen dances. Last show I got to meet David King."

"Wow," crooned Carol. "David King! What was he like?"

Bren shrugged her shoulders. She was not the type to be impressed easily, especially if someone thought she *should* be impressed.

"He wasn't anything special, just an ordinary person. Actually he was a little shy offstage."

"Ordinary or not, I'd give anything to meet him and a number of other musicians I can think of, like that lead singer for the group that's going to play at the Spring Dance, The Blasters."

Just as Carol finished her sentence, all our heads turned at the sound of Mrs. MacDonald's office door opening.

My heart dropped when Mrs. MacDonald said to Carol, "Well, Carol, you just may get that opportunity sooner than you dreamed."

Bren and I looked at each other. Her face was full of sympathy. We were both thinking the same thing. Carol had gotten the position.

But then Mrs. MacDonald turned to me and said, "Maggie, thanks for waiting around this afternoon because I've got good news for both you and Carol. During the initial interviews, I realized that two models would be more efficient than one. What if the only Petite model got sick or had other commitments on the day of a show? So, I convinced Mr. Farland to allow me to select two new Board members. So, Carol, Maggie, welcome aboard. I think the two of you will make wonderful representatives for girls your size."

I don't think either of us could believe our ears. Both of us? That would take some getting used to, the two of *us* working together. I could tell by the stunned expression on Carol's face that she was having the same thoughts.

Dismissing for the moment the surprise of sharing my new position, I considered the fact that I'd actually done it: My dream had come true!

But Mrs. MacDonald wasn't finished. Looking at Carol, she said, "I hope not too many Board members have engagements they can't break for the evening of Ridgeway's Spring Dance. I just completed an agreement with the school to conduct a spring fashion show in between the Blasters' sets."

"The Blasters—oh, wow!" drooled Carol.

"I'm hoping to have you both show-ready by then," she continued, turning toward me. "And Maggie, I probably don't have to remind you that next Saturday is also the evening of your 16th birthday." I nodded my head attentively. What could she be getting at?

"If you would prefer to skip that show, I'd certainly understand. Remember, that's one of the reasons there's two of you. To allow a certain measure of flexibility."

No way was I going to let Carol have the show entirely to herself. People would think she was the new member, then when I showed up later on, they'd suppose I was second choice, a backup to Carol.

"Oh, no, Mrs. MacDonald. I was just planning on going to the dance anyway."

Didn't I see a flash of disappointment flicker across Carol's face?

"Well, in that case, Maggie, I'm afraid you're still going to have to disappoint some young man when you break your date for the evening. Unfortunately, you girls are likely to miss out on a good share of the actual dance," she told us.

I could feel myself turning red, embarrassed by Mrs. MacDonald's assumption that I already had a date for the dance. Naturally, Carol spoke out, saying, "Yes, *my* date will be disappointed."

It wasn't until that minute that I realized that from my point of view, there *was* something lucky about sharing the title with Carol. Now she wouldn't be attending the dance as Matt's date!

And so maybe, just maybe, I would get the chance I dreamed of, the chance to dance with one Matt Brennan on the night of my 16th birthday.

6

Before she returned to her inner office, Mrs. MacDonald described briefly the week-long crash modeling course that we'd begin on Monday right after school. She gave both Carol and me her congratulations and then left the three of us girls uncomfortably alone.

Bren told Carol congratulations, Carol and I told each other congratulations, and then Carol said she had some shopping to do and left Bren and me to ourselves.

The minute Carol was out of sight, I burst out with the biggest smile possible and Bren opened her arms wide for a congratulatory hug.

"I knew it! I knew you'd get on!" she told me.

Personally, I hadn't known. And so now, I was so pent up with excess nervous energy that I felt like hollering at the top of my lungs. My earlier calmness escaped me, transforming itself into a surging power that made me feel like Superwoman herself.

"I'll meet you at the car," I told Bren, somewhat abruptly. I had to get moving, to disperse some of my new superstrength.

"Hey, wait up," called Bren, as she watched me take the down escalator two steps at a time. "This is a respectable department store. You represent this place now. You know, there's an image to be upheld!" she chided. But by then, I was already flying out the store's front doors, galloping along in my tight skirt like an awkward penguin toward Bren's Volkswagen.

Waiting for Bren to catch up with me, I had time alone to comtemplate the ramifications of my new position. Would, as Carol had suggested, boys find me more attractive now? Would one of them ask me out on a date?

Suddenly my excitement began to give away to fear. For the first time in my life, I'd gone after something on my own, something *I* wanted, not something a parent or other adult wanted for me. And I'd succeeded.

Succeeded as far as I'd gone, that is. Actually my responsibilities were only beginning. And I couldn't rely on Dad, or even Bren, to help me. I was on my own.

So when Bren came walking toward me with her self-assured, purposeful stride, big alligator tears welled up in my eyes. I knew they wouldn't escape Bren's discerning eye.

"You silly. You made it. Why are you crying?"

She reached out to hug me, gradually turning it into a bear hug, squeezing so tightly that I started coughing. Of course, this made us both crack up, which is what Bren had in mind all along. My tears were forgotten.

"With my best friend along, the fashion shows will be so much more fun," said Bren as we climbed into Betsy. "And just think, we get paid too."

With all the excitement of just making it, I'd forgotten even to think about the fringe benefits like having some money of my own and not having to ask Dad for spending money all the time.

"I still can't believe I really made it," I told Bren as she maneuvered Betsy into the moving lane or traffic. "Me—the original shrimp—a model. It'll take a while for all of this to sink in." I thought for just a minute and then asked her, "Bren, would you mind if we headed straight for my house?"

If I knew Bren, she'd have already begun thinking up some celebration plans. Not only was I anxious to tell Dad the news, I needed some time alone, as well.

"Don't worry, I know how you're feeling right now," Bren reassured me. "Real otherworldly, right? Remember how weird I was last summer when I found out I'd made it? I promptly splurged on a whole quart of Baskin-Robbins ice cream. I got so sick I barely made it to the welcoming ceremony the next day. I still can't stomach the sight of chocolate-mint ice cream."

"So that's what was wrong with you! I wondered why you didn't come over to see me that night. In fact, I remember thinking that maybe you were going to get real stuck-up because of your new position."

We laughed together, luxuriating in the cruise down a familiar street, with Betsy's windows rolled down all the way, and the radio turned up loud. Bren and I, along with Michael Jackson and Paul McCartney, sang, "The girl is mine . . . No, she's mine . . . No, no, she's mine . . . ."

Bren and I pulled up just as Dad was backing the Bronco out of the carport.

"Dad, wait up," I called, jumping out of Betsy to waylay him. The puppies heard my voice and started jumping around in the back end of the Bronco. "I made it. I'm a model!"

Dad parked immediately and jumped out to give me a big hug. After his previous reticence, I was relieved to see that he seemed genuinely happy for me.

"Maggie, I'm really proud of you." Then sporting a mischievous grin, he said, "Now you're certain you're not going to consider yourself too big-time for your regular-folk dad?"

"Oh, Dad," I said, laughing and giving his shoulder a playful shove.

By now, the puppies were going wild, their tails wagging ferociously, not at all happy about missing out on the attention Dad and I were giving each other. Cherub let out a little bark, as though to say, "Hey, you guys, remember me?"

His strategy worked. We all looked his way and then Dad asked me, "Maggie, how about dogsitting Cookie while Cherub and I visit Dr. Hill?"

Suddenly I got goose bumps all up and down my spine. On previous appointments, Cookie had always gone along with Cherub. Why didn't Dad want to take her this time?

I told myself that Dad probably figured I'd enjoy some company while he was gone to help keep me from floating off into space. I'm sure that my excitement about landing the Board position was impossibly obvious. I couldn't remember a time I'd felt as happy.

"Sure, Dad, Cookie can stay at home with me. I was just planning on hanging around the house for the afternoon, anyway. You know, kind of let the reality of the situation sink in."

"I think I know how you're feeling, honey," Dad said as he stepped up next to me and put a fatherly arm around my shoulder. "I will *never* forget the day I made Marshfield's Debate Team."

Somehow—don't ask me how—Bren and I managed to hold back our laughter until Dad had driven off.

"Can you believe it?" I asked Bren. "How could he possibly compare the Fashion Board to a debate team?" I reminded myself that Dad was only doing his best to be an understanding father.

Bren stuck around for a little while, then she had to leave to get ready for her date with Randy that evening.

"Wish I'd thought to leave tonight open. You and I should be celebrating tonight," she told me.

"That's OK, Bren. I need to spend some time with Dad and the puppies anyway. Starting Monday, I'm going to be so busy they'll have to make appointments to see me."

"Actually I don't think you know the half of it. You've got a lot to learn in a week's time."

I knew she was right. That's why at first the idea of just lounging around the house for the rest of the afternoon seemed appealing. But soon after Bren had left, the bright sunshine outside and the super adrenalin charge I felt inside made me change my mind.

Obviously I couldn't announce to the whole world how fantastically fortunate I was, but I decided I could at least venture out into that world and perhaps let it see for itself that there was a new Maggie Williams in town.

Cookie and I headed up the stairs to my room so I could change into clothes more suitable for a bike ride. A ride along the bike path to Lake Hood enticed me; it sounded like a good way to work off some of my restless exictement.

I pulled on my favorite jeans and a short-sleeved, maroon T-shirt that has a picture of a white unicorn and pink sparkling letters that spell "UNIQUE" across the front. Then I lifted my hair into a high ponytail, rolled up a maroon and aqua paisley scarf, and wrapped it around my head, tying the loose ends around my ponytail.

Studying the effects in my full-length mirror, a girl's best friend and worst enemy, I decided that my new make-up job needed some repair work. Without practice, I knew I wouldn't be able to duplicate the wonderful illusions Sheri had created with a couple of shades of lavender eye shadow and two tones of pink blush, but I figured I could at least eliminate some of the emerging black smudges from beneath both eyes.

After I'd done what I could, I stood back to appraise the final product. I stared at my face as though it belonged to someone else. That's when it struck me how first impressions are almost always formed on the basis of a person's appearance.

What had been Matt's first impressions of me? And how would those impressions change now that I'd gained the prestige of becoming a member of the Fashion Board?

I gave my reflection a scolding frown. Why waste my time worrying about Matt's impressions of me, anyway? So what if Carol couldn't be his date at the Spring Dance. That wouldn't stop them from getting together.

Suddenly angry at myself for letting the gorgeous afternoon sun slip away while I talked to myself in the mirror, I made a stupid-looking face, then watched as my reflection laughed back at me. Meanwhile, Cookie waited for me patiently, cocking her head sideways to give me a funny look that said: "I'll never understand humans!"

When I started to tie my tennies, she lost control. With her behind wiggling and eyes glistening with excitement, Cookie ran off ahead of me toward the front door. When I arrived I found her with her nose shoved against the crack in the doorway as though she intended to squeeze right through if I didn't hurry up and open it for her.

Out on the bike trail, I wasn't the only one braving the nippy air for a chance to bask in the brilliant spring sunlight. Every once in a while, Cookie ran off to chase one of the other bike riders or a jogger but for a five-month-old puppy, she was exceptionally obedient. At least, that was my opinion at the time.

Even before Lake Hood came into sight, the loud buzz of float planes announced the lake's proximity. Harold Brenski's speech about Alaskan aviation came back to me—hadn't he told us that Lake Hood was the busiest float-plane lake in the entire United States? And somewhere I'd heard that the waiting list for a mooring on the lake was endless.

Because it was a Saturday, the lake buzzed with activity. All along the water's edge, people were busy dewinterizing their planes. Many were changing over from skis or wheels to floats; others were tinkering with engines or simply washing and waxing.

I noticed that Cookie, too, seemed affected by the approaching hustle and bustle. The reason was apparent. From the number of dogs I saw running around the lake, pilots were great admirers of man's best friend.

Noticeably absent, however, were humans of the female species, most of the aviators were men. If Bren had been along, she'd have pointed out that this was prime man-hunting territory. I smiled to myself, again observing that all of a sudden everything I thought about seemed to have something to do with boys. Had that perilous affliction "boy craziness" finally claimed me as a victim?

Before I had time to confirm the diagnosis, my attention was suddenly riveted back to the real world by my mischievous puppy. Cookie had spotted a young black Labrador retriever and enticed him into a game of chase. They romped round and round a green-and-white Super Cub whose owner was balanced precariously atop a too-short step ladder. The short, round man's head was buried deep inside the plane's engine.

I opened my mouth, but it was already too late. Cookie led her unsuspecting playmate underneath the man's ladder. Cookie fit, but the Lab didn't. The ladder and its occupant came crashing down, the latter with a solid thud.

I stopped my bike about 50 feet away. The darkening crimson color on the little man's face told me that, in this case, a diplomatic explanation or apology was not a viable option. The situation demanded nothing short of a full retreat.

"Cookie, come!"

This time, she decided to obey. However she was still so wound up from her games with the black Lab that even when she'd gotten back on the trail, she didn't slow down.

Up ahead, the bike path was very straight, so I leaned forward, flattening myself against the handle bars and proceeded to give it my all. I pumped like crazy, trying to catch up with Cookie who was now a considerable distance in front of me.

Not until I'd soared past several other cyclists did I realize that my speed had accelerated dangerously because of a slight downgrade to the trail.

When at last Cookie stopped to look back at her mistress, she probably got one of the biggest scares of her young life. From her vantage point, I must have looked like a lean, mean, speeding machine ready to mow her down.

Panic-stricken, Cookie ran off the trail toward the lake. After a near-collision with some cute guy carrying a pail of water, she ran right back across the bike path, just at the moment that I reached the same intersection.

My first thought as I went flying through the air was that I'd run over and probably mutilated my puppy. Then I landed and forgot about everything but myself.

I suppose I was lucky to have gone sailing off the side of the trail, landing in the muddy, wet muck rather than on the blacktopped bike trail. I came down hands first—a stupid move that could have broken both my wrists—but because the ground was at its breakup best, I landed in a spot as soft and sloppy as a pig's sty.

After a couple of minutes of just trying to comprehend my situation, the first thing I saw was that the boy Cookie had almost run into was rushing over to help me. Self-conscious about my disheveled appearance, a cute boy was the last person I wanted as an eyewitness. I was so busy being embarrassed that I didn't look up at my would-be rescuer until the very last minute, when I heard him say:

"Are you hurt?"

I wished that I *had* been hurt a little, then at least then I'd have had an excuse important enough to divert his attention from my graceless exhibition. But since I wasn't I concentrated on thinking up a suitably bright and witty reply for the stranger.

When I looked up and saw his face, very near to my own mud-covered one, all I could do was spit and sputter and finally I actually began choking out loud.

The cute boy kneeling down beside me was Matt Brennan!

7

The minute I recognized that it was Matt bending over me, I remembered Bren's telling me about Matt having an uncle with an airplane on Lake Hood. No doubt I subconsciously chose this particular bike trail.

I hoped that didn't imply that my subconscious had gone so far as to plan this opportune little accident. That was too much to believe, seeing as I must have looked like some swamp-born creature as I emerged haltingly from the mud. Not exactly the most glamorous appearance for a young and upcoming new model!

"Maggie! That *is* you, isn't it?"

"Afraid so," I answered, embarrassed to admit it. Actually, I should have been getting used to it by then. Seeing as how every time I'd ever come in contact with Matt, I found myself in the middle of an embarrassing situation.

First there had been the collision in the hall and then the confrontation with Mr. Knoll over my application. The only difference this time was that no third party was involved. Unless you counted Cookie, that is. But basically, this time it was a one-on-one situation with our facing each other alone.

"Are you hurt?" he asked gently, as he helped me to my feet.

"I'm not sure . . . I don't think so," I concluded, successfully managing to take a few steps on my own.

"You look to me as if you're still all in one piece," he offered.

"How could you possibly tell *what* kind of condition I'm in underneath all this mud?" I teased back at him. Then I remembered the reason behind the entire situation.

"Oh, no. Where's Cookie?" I cried. As I began looking frantically in every direction for my forgotten, possibly hurt puppy, Matt tapped me on the shoulder, pointed toward the lake, and said, "Is that what you're looking for?"

I spotted Cookie running alongside a black and brown, nondescript, medium-sized dog. They splashed along the small strip of melting ice that bordered the lake's shore.

"Is that other dog yours, Matt?"

"Sure is. Her name's Jam, short for Just A Mutt. You don't have to worry about your puppy, she's in good hands. Jam won't let her run off."

"I wouldn't be so sure about that. Did you happen to witness how my accident occurred in the first place?" I asked him.

"Afraid so. That Cookie of yours was really moving."

"So was I. I thought for sure I'd squashed her," I told him, looking over at the two rambunctious canines.

"Doesn't look as if she's too worried about it. I'd say you should be more concerned about yourself. You sure you're OK?"

"Of course." Actually, I was so preoccupied with carrying on an intelligent conversation, I hadn't noticed the goose bumps crawling up and down my arm.

"You're cold, Maggie," he told me sternly. "Come on, let's get you inside my truck where you can warm up."

Worried that my puppy would think I'd abandoned her if I disappeared inside Matt's truck, I looked toward the lake to check on her. But now the two dogs lay side by side in a circle of sunshine, passed out, completely oblivious to the rest of the world.

"OK, I guess I am getting a little chilly," I conceded, thinking to myself that at least the shivers would disguise how nervous I was over the idea of getting asked to climb inside *his* pickup.

Matt walked me around to the passenger's side and opened the door for me. When I saw the spotless interior, I changed my mind.

"I'll get your upholstery all muddy!" I protested.

"It'll wash," he replied nonchalantly, taking my hand to help support me as I climbed up into the tall rig. I guess sometimes being short has its advantages, after all.

Then he walked back around to the driver's side, climbed in, and started the engine so that the heater would warm up. I felt rather wimpy sitting inside a pickup truck with the heater running full blast on the nicest day of the year. I appreciated the warmth, though, and Matt and I had a perfect view of the lake, the dogs, and lots of airplanes.

"Is that your uncle's plane you're working on?" I asked, looking at a blue-and-white, four-passenger aircraft parked out in front of us.

"Yeah. I was just giving it a good spring cleanup job. But, how'd you know I had an uncle with an airplane?"

Me and my big mouth. "Oh-oh," I said meekly. Then I realized what an ideal opportunity I had to show Matt what kind of person Carol really was. "There's a little birdie flying around Ridgeway who's been saying that you're a pilot and that you fly your uncle's plane a lot." No point telling him that I'd also known *where* his uncle's plane was parked. I didn't want Matt to think *I* was chasing him.

"I see," he answered, his voice exhibiting total noncommittal. He had to know it was Carol to whom I was referring, but when he didn't show any interest in pursuing the subject, I decided I'd better try a different approach.

"How long have you been flying, Matt? I've never even been up in a little plane." I'd always wanted to but had never had the opportunity.

"Really? I go up every chance I get. Uncle Charlie pays me for the work I do on his plane with free flying hours. I'm lucky to have such a great uncle."

I noticed a look of wistfulness in Matt's eyes as he stared at his uncle's plane. Suddenly I realized that I'd quite abruptly interrupted his after-noon and whatever plans he'd had for himself. So I asked, "Hey, were you going flying when you finished your job? If so, I'll get going so you don't waste away your whole afternoon."

Looking out at the beautiful blue skies, I thought to myself what a perfect day it was for flying, and how utterly fantastic it would be if Matt were to say to me, "Come on, why don't you go flying with me?" But apparently the thought didn't occur to him.

"Oh, no, Maggie. No flying today. It'll take me all afternoon to get her spiffed up. Uncle Charlie and I plan to go up tomorrow."

After that, I didn't have to worry about lags in the conversation. For at least the next half an hour, Matt talked about nothing but how much he loved to fly and how much he envied his uncle's courageous flying adventures.

"Uncle Charlie used to be a bush pilot," he explained.

"A what kind of pilot?" I asked, wishing I'd paid better attention to Harold Brenski's speech.

"A pilot who flies the wilds of Alaska. One time, back in the early '50s, Uncle Charlie saved a whole Eskimo village by delivering a lifesaving serum through a blizzard everyone said would be impossible to navigate.

"Wow! No wonder you respect him so much."

"He's quite a pilot, all right," agreed Matt. Once again, I caught a glimmer of that faraway look in Matt's eyes. It was obvious that flying would always be his first love. I couldn't help wondering if perhaps there could be room in his affections for me too.

"But listen," said Matt, turning to face me, "we've been talking about what I like to do all this time. How about if you talk for a while. How'd that interview go anyway? Did you get the modeling job?"

"It's not really a job," I told him. "It's a position on Farland's Fashion Board. It does involve some modeling, but we have to work in the store and participate in community activities sponsored by Farland's, as well."

"OK, so let me rephrase my question: Did you get the position?"

At first I couldn't understand why it was taking me so long to share the news that earlier I'd wanted to shout out to the world. Then it dawned on me. I knew subconsciously that I'd have to bring Carol into our conversation again, and this time I couldn't get away with not using her name.

"Yes, I got it." Time for the whole truth. "But I tied."

"What? With whom?"

I thought for a minute and realized that surely Matt knew that Carol was an applicant too. I mean, he couldn't have spent all evening with her at the Super Duper without her at least mentioning it to him.

"Oh, you know, one of those 'upperclassmen,'" I said lightly, certain he'd catch on.

"So she made it too, huh? You two ought to make quite a team," he teased.

I decided that diplomacy was definitely one of Matt's better assets. Thus far, I hadn't been able to determine to what extent Matt cared for Carol. Although he was acting warm and friendly toward me, we both knew that thus far he'd spent most of his brief time at Ridgeway in her company. Was Carol shoving herself on him without his approval or was he the willing recipient? I decided to see if I could find out, if I could make him come across in a definite manner about something besides airplanes.

"From what I've heard, you and Carol are the ones who're making quite a team."

From the expression of surprise on his face, I decided that at last I was getting somewhere. The question I forgot to ask myself was: *Will it be where I wanted to go?*

"What are you talking about, Maggie?"

Still hedging, I thought. so I spelled it out for him.

"Oh, just that Ridgeway rumor has it that she asked you to next Saturday's dance." He sat there wordless, waiting for me to go on. "And you accepted."

"Boy! This may be the Last Frontier, but news sure travels at an uptown pace, doesn't it?"

So it was true! He intended to go to the Spring Dance with Carol. I'd asked for it, but now I was sorry I'd brought it up at all, because, from then on, I found it difficult to talk to Matt without picturing the two of them together.

I suddenly didn't feel so well. I wanted to get away from Matt, to go home, and get out of my mud-soaked clothing and into a shower.

Also, for the first time since Cookie and I had left the house, it occurred to me to wonder how late it was getting. Anxious to hear Dr. Hill's latest diagnosis, I'd planned to arrive back home before Dad and Cherub. I couldn't believe it when I looked down at my watch.

"Oh! I've got to get going. I didn't know how late it was."

"What's the hurry?"

"My dad took Cookie's brother, Cherub, to the vet this afternoon." I considered how much to tell him. "He's pretty sick."

"Oh, I'm sorry, Maggie." The sincerity in Matt's voice suggested that another asset of Matt's was that he cared deeply for animals. He was genuinely concerned for the health of a puppy he'd never seen. Apparently Matt loved animals almost as much as he loved flying.

"I've got it! Why don't I load Cookie and your bike into the back of my pickup and drive you home? Save you a lot of time," he added convincingly.

Sometimes I swear there is a little gremlin inside me that maliciously destroys my best opportunities. Because instead of accepting his offer, what I heard myself saying was, "Thanks anyway, Matt, but we don't live far away. Besides, didn't your uncle hire you to get a job done?"

Matt looked me right in the eyes and said, "You're right. Thanks for reminding me. I'd forgotten all about working." Then he gave me one of those heart-melting smiles of his and said, "But I really do think we owe it to ourselves to get together again, OK?"

"OK." I was unconvinced of the likelihood, however.

Without waiting for him to go around and open it for me, I opened the pickup door and jumped out. I walked stiffly toward my bike, turning once to wave good-bye. Cookie saw me departing and tore out across the grass to join me.

As I pedaled off toward home, I thought about what it was that had made me say no to Matt's generous offer.

For one thing, I told myself, Dad would have been suspicious at the sight of my riding home with a stranger, especially in my present state of disarray.

Secondly, I was only trying my best to be realistic about the situation. Why get my hopes up over a boy when he'd already committed himself so willingly to another girl?

Even so, remembering his parting words, I was powerless to prevent a shimmering sliver of hope from entering my heart.

8

By the time Cookie and I made it home, Dad was sitting in his easy chair, reading the evening paper. I prepared myself for the inevitable question-and-answer period over how I'd gotten so filthy, but when he lifted his head to greet me, he didn't even seem to notice my mud-stained clothing. The look on his face told me right away that something was wrong. And when I didn't see any evidence of Cherub, I panicked.

"Where's Cherub?" I asked him in a voice full of accusation.

"Now, Maggie, hold on just a minute, he's OK. Dr. Hill took Cherub home with him for the rest of the weekend to observe the little guy's condition firsthand.

"So when's he coming home?"

"I'm meeting Dr. Hill at his office first thing Monday morning. He'll give me a complete evaluation of Cherub's problem then."

Even though he sat in the room's most comfortable chair, Dad looked unusually ill at ease.

"Maggie, honey, listen now. Dr. Hill never came right out and said so, but I got the distinct impression that he fears Cherub's condition may not be treatable."

"What do you mean, not treatable?"

What I saw in his eyes was the same kind of message for which Dad had had to pull me out of school in the middle of the day—the day Mom died.

"No!" I shouted. "What right does Dr. Hill have to decide something like that? Lots of handicapped people live happy, productive lives. Maybe Cherub would rather be a handicapped dog than no dog at all."

"Maggie, please get control of yourself and listen to me for a minute. We're not talking about a handicap; we're talking about a progressively debilitating disease."

"Like Mom's."

"Similar inasmuch as the doctor's ability to cure Cherub's illness is limited."

Sensing that something was wrong, Cookie came up to me and nuzzled her way into my lap. Dad focused his eyes on her as he spoke.

"I'm sorry the timing is so bad, sweetheart. You don't know how much I dreaded spoiling your day of celebration. Please remember, I'm just as anxious as you that Cherub receive the best possible care. Dr. Hill is going out of his way to do everything he can to help Cherub recover."

Suddenly I realized how selfishly I was acting. This had to be harder on Dad than me. After all, we were talking about Dad's puppy, not mine.

Cherub and Dad had taken to each other right from the start. Standing a short distance from the pack of eight puppies on the day we'd gone to choose *one*, Dad had put two fingers in his mouth and let loose a sharp, clear whistle. Most of the puppies had turned their heads and lifted their floppy little ears at the sound. The others ignored Dad completely, except for Cherub who came bounding down the hill without hesitation, heading straight for Dad.

Dad had picked Cherub up and said to me, "Well, Maggie, I've chosen my puppy. What's taking you so long?"

"You mean we get to take two of them home?" I cried with delight.

Dad decided to name his puppy Cherub after the angels, because he was so sure Mom was among them. Ever since that day, Dad seemed more lighthearted, more ready to face a future without Mom.

So now, as I sat and looked at the sorrowful lines in Dad's face, I realized that his affection for Cherub stretched beyond the love a man would have had for an ordinary puppy.

"Oh, Dad, I'm sorry for being such a baby."

I leaned over and gave him a big hug. By the way his arms reached out to encircle me, I knew that he needed comforting just as much as I did.

"Now, young lady, how about if you explain your condition of filthiness?"

I figured he'd notice sooner or later. So I gave him a rundown on Cookie's and my adventures at the lake—from the humorous fall of the fat man to a noncommittal version of my bike crash and how the person who helped me happened to be the new boy at school. When I mentioned that he and his family had moved to Anchorage from Portland, Dad asked me for Matt's last name.

"Brennan? Your mother used to have a girl friend with that name; I wonder if they're any relation. We ought to do something neighborly sometime soon, have them over for coffee some evening."

If Mom were alive, the invitation would have been swift and for a full meal. At least Dad appeared to be thinking along more sociable lines; a year ago he'd never have even thought of the coffee idea.

I was just heading up the stairs to get out of my dirty clothes and into a shower when the phone rang. When Dad hollered up that it was for me, I figured it was Bren calling before she left on her date with Randy. We usually talked to each other at least a couple of times a day on the weekends, and since this wasn't any ordinary weekend, I felt sure she was calling up to congratulate me again.

So I finished getting undressed and got into my robe before I trudged back down the stairs to talk to her. Dad was still standing beside the phone table, holding the receiver in his hand, wearing a mischievous grin. I knew right away it was someone besides Bren but I didn't dare think about who I hoped it would be. I took the phone, shooed Dad off, then lifted the receiver to my ear.

"Hi, Maggie, it's me, Matt. I just thought I'd give you a call to see that you made it home without any more mishaps. Hope I didn't catch you at a bad time."

"Oh, no. Cookie and I got home fine. I was just getting cleaned up," I confessed, embarrassed by how long I'd made him wait for me. I hoped he had more conversation in mind than that because it was all I could to come up with answers. His call had turned me upside down, inside out, and made everything in me tremble, including my voice. I'm talking about an absolutely total state of shock!

"I also wanted to find out if your other puppy, Cherub, if he's going to be OK."

I gathered my forces to compose a functional answer. It registered in my mind what a completely thoughtful person Matt was to show such concern for a dog he'd never even met.

"Dr. Hill is keeping him for observation over the weekend. The doctor said he'd decide by Monday what he thinks his prognosis will be."

"Boy, sounds real serious. What'd you say he has?"

"It's called hip dysplasia." I choked on the words.

"Wow, I'm really sorry, Maggie."

For the next minute or two, which seemed like forever, I suffered unbearably as we suddenly ran out of conversation. Matt was silent and I couldn't think of a thing to say. Still I kept getting the feeling that Matt had another, unspoken reason for calling me. For once I was right.

"Listen, Maggie, I was looking at the evening paper just before I called you and I noticed that they're showing a film on Alaska tonight over at the university. I was thinking, well, I used to catch some pretty good flicks at the university back in Portland. . . ."

"I've been there! The three of us used to go there to see old movies, foreign films . . . you know."

"Right! So I was wondering, if you aren't real busy, I know this is short notice and all, but would you like to go check out the movie with me?"

"Tonight?" Yes, dummy, that's what he said, wasn't it? When at last my nervous system registered that a minor miracle had just occurred, my knees buckled and I slid down the wall to the floor. Matt was asking me out!

"Eight o'clock is show time. I could pick you up at 7:30, if that's all right with you."

"Oh, that will be fine, Matt."

Sure, that'll be just fine, I told myself. Here I am, a total disaster. I have to get my hair washed and dried and curled, not to mention picking out something to wear and then trying to do my face, all in less than two hours.

"What did you say the movie was about?" I asked, thinking of Dad. He'd want all the details. Not that I'd blame him. After all, this would be my first real date.

"I get the idea it's mostly wilderness scenes of Alaska, taken from an airplane similar to my uncle's. Guess I should have asked you if you're even interested in the outdoors."

"Oh, yes, I love the outdoors. Well, except for strategically placed mud puddles," I joked.

"Right," he said laughing with me. "Well, I'd better get going. Mom's got dinner ready."

For just a second, I thought about Mom, thinking how sad it was that I could never again make that same statement. But the ache inside was brief and no longer so painful, and behind it came a deep, flowing river of love and appreciation for everything she'd ever done or been, and for the love she'd bestowed upon Dad and me.

"OK, see you at 7:30," I told him. Willing the strength to return to my knees, I pushed myself back up the wall into a standing position.

And that's where I stayed until Dad showed up a few minutes later—leaning against the wall, a glazed-over expression on my face.

"Maggie, are you all right? Who was it? What did he want?"

"That was Matt Brennan, the new boy I told you about. He wants to take me to a movie at the university tonight and no, I'm not all right! Dad . . . I'm going on a date!"

In my state of hypnotic frenzy, I forgot to take Dad's feelings into consideration. Believe me, he reminded me without hesitation.

"Maggie, you're going nowhere . . . with no boy . . . without my permission. Obviously you did not take that into consideration when you made your plans." With that, he turned his back on me and stormed off toward the living room. It was clear that if I were entertaining the hope of changing his mind, I would have to follow.

"Dad, what's the big deal? Matt is a nice boy and I finally get asked out and by a boy that I've been dreaming of since the day I first met him. And you don't want to give me permission to go? I can't believe it!"

"Now, Maggie, let's back up here a minute. It's not true that I do not want to give you permission to go on the date. But I fully expected at least to have been consulted before a decision was agreed upon."

"You mean I should have asked you before I said yes?"

"Precisely."

"And what would you have said if I had asked?" Believe it or not, I began to smile because I knew my Dad so well. I *had* been wrong not to ask his permission, I realized that immediately. I'd been so overwhelmed by the fact that Matt actually was asking me out that I forgot about anything else. But I also knew Dad was a softie who trusted my judgment and who most likely would have said yes anyway.

"I would have asked you what movie you planned to attend, when it started, and when you intended to be back home. And whether you truly trusted this boy you've only known a short while."

"And I would have told you that the movie starts at 8:00, we'll be home at whatever time you deem reasonable, and, yes, I truly trust Matt; even Bren likes him," I added, suddenly realizing that she would flip out when I told her the news, which, of course, now I was dying to do. But I was also acutely aware that the tiny amount of time allotted me to transform myself into Cinderella was ticking away. Where is a girl's fairy godmother when she needs her?

"Well, I probably would have said yes and, under the circumstances, I will say yes, with the provision that I have ultimate veto rights if I hate the guy on sight," he said, only half-teasing. I just laughed, assuring him that he had nothing to worry about, that he'd like Matt immediately.

I grabbed a quick sandwich—that had been Dad's only other stipulation: that I eat something before I went out, a reasonable request since I'd had no dinner. But I really didn't like giving up the precious time. After that, I stole another few minutes to give Bren a quick call to tell her I was going on a date with Matt Brennan.

"Maggie, that's wonderful! How'd you do it?"

I considered my answer for a moment and then told her, "The direct approach. I tried to run him down with my bicycle."

"You did what? Wait a minute. I only dropped you off a few hours ago. What's been going on? You said you were going to stay home all afternoon."

"Well, I had a change of heart," I said, relishing the expression because it seemed to say so much. "Listen, Bren, I don't have time to explain right now, Matt will be here soon. Call me tomorrow. Oh, I forgot. Dad and I are going down to Portage Glacier for the day, so I'll call you when we get back."

Like me, Bren prefers to sleep late. I knew Dad would want to get an early start, so I didn't offer to wake her with a call before we left. She didn't suggest it, either.

"OK, but I'll be dying to know what happened both today and tonight!"

I was pretty curious about how the evening would turn out myself. "Act naturally" were Bren's last words of advice before she hung up. I repeated them over and over while I tried to get ready on time.

I finally decided on my lavender cotton pants and pink-and-lavender-striped top. I was still repeating Bren's motto and curling my hair when the doorbell rang. I looked at the clock and saw that Matt was right on time. I knew I'd be a little late, but that would give Dad the time he needed to scope Matt out. I figured Matt could handle my father, and if he couldn't, well, we might as well find out right away.

But I was absolutely correct about the two of them hitting it off, as I discovered when I came down the stairs a few minutes later.

"Maggie! Did you know that Matt's folks and I went to the same high school, only a few years' difference?" He turned to Matt and asked, "Say, does your dad have a sister a couple of years older than he?"

"Aunt Molly. She lives in California," answered Matt.

Nervous that Dad might keep Matt there talking all night, I decided to hurry things up a little. "Sorry, Dad, we've got to go or we'll be late for the movie."

"Oh, of course, you two run along now. What time did you say you'd have her home, son?"

"Well, the show will let out around ten. I thought we'd get a bite to eat and then come home."

Dad nodded his approval. "You two have a good time."

There was no question in my mind that we'd have anything but the very best of times together. And, I hoped, for more than just one evening.

9

We walked into the theater just as the show began. Matt had been right. Most of the movie was filmed from an airplane so that the audience got a firsthand experience of the feeling of flying in the plane themselves.

"I was hoping that's what it would be like," Matt told me later at the Super Duper over fries and chocolate shakes. "Since you've never been up in a small plane, I wanted you to get an advance idea of the experience. Think you'd like the real thing?"

I didn't admit it to Matt, but the first few turns and dips of the small plane flying alongside the jagged glaciers had made my stomach do flipflops. But after a while, that slight airsick sensation lessened as I became engrossed in the movie's spectacular scenery.

"I think I'm going to love it. When do I get to find out?"

Matt's face changed and I knew I'd overstepped a boundary. He seemed flustered, almost embarrassed. Finally he answered, "Oh . . . one of these days, Maggie. I'll let you know." Then he changed the subject, marveling over the enormous salmon and trout to be had in Alaska's bush country.

"My uncle and I are planning a fly-out fishing trip one of these days this spring. He says I'll catch trout the size of Oregon salmon. I think he's exaggerating, but I'm willing to find out firsthand."

We talked for a while about various places and experiences we had in common from spending our youth in the same city. We'd lived on oppo-site sides of town, and thus far had discovered no common acquain-tances, but even sharing a knowledge of the same town and its landmarks created the feeling that we'd grown up together.

"You know that ivy-covered brick building right across from where they always held the movies we both used to go to? Well, that's where my dad taught most of his classes."

"I remember the one you mean. From its turn-of-the-century archi-tecture, I'd say it's one of the university's oldest buildings, probably built about the same time as my old high school, talking about ancient hal-lowed halls!"

"I'd heard Rosewood was the pits," I said, sympathetically.

"Now hold on a minute. I wouldn't go that far. I had some really great times at Rosewood." Matt's voice sounded defensive, and I could see that he missed his old friends.

"I'm sorry, Matt. I didn't mean it that way. I guess it came out pretty snooty!" *I probably sounded as bratty as Carol*, I thought to myself. "But that's what all the kids at my school used to say."

"I know. And there *were* a lot of rank kids at Rosewood. My old girl friend, for one."

Now this was a surprising turn in the conversation, but at least we were on what I considered the right track—what it took to become Matt Bren-nan's girl friend.

"Oh?" I asked, with polite but offhand interest. "Why do you say that?"

"Because Cindy was the biggest flirt and two-timer that ever lived." Bit-terness leaped from his tongue. I was seeing a different side of Matt. "She used to do things to make me jealous on purpose. And, boy, did I get jealous! She used to turn me into a crazy man. I didn't figure out until just before we moved that she did it because she wanted to feel loved."

"She sounds like a very unhappy person inside."

"You're right. You know, I wouldn't tell this to just anybody, but Carol reminds me a lot of my old girl friend."

Oh, great, I thought to myself. No wonder Matt seemed naturally attracted and comfortable with Carol. She was the same kind of girl he had obviously fallen head over heels for back home.

"They even look a lot alike," Matt continued. Hallelujah, I praised silently. I could see right then that I could never expect to match up to Matt's expectations of a girl's looks. Whatever was he doing sitting here with me?

Then just as suddenly as it had arrived, Matt lost that faraway look in his gorgeous eyes and said, "I'm sorry, Maggie. How uncouth of me to talk about girl friends on our first date."

First, I told myself with joy, *first as in the first of many more!* "That's OK," I told him, using my best voice of understanding. "I remember how alone I felt when we first moved to Anchorage. Even after two years, sometimes I still feel like an outsider."

"I find that hard to believe," Matt said kindly. "Really, Maggie, I had no right to go off on such a tangent. It's just that it seems as if you and I have known each other for more than just a week."

I wanted to tell him I felt exactly the same way but all I could do was nod my head.

"Well, I guess I'd better get the professor's daughter home on time if I don't want to flunk out on our first date. Ready?"

I slurped up the last of my shake and grabbed my coat. Matt reached out and took it from me so he could help me into it. He was every bit the gentleman I'd imagined.

Later that evening after Matt had delivered me home safely, I snuggled down under my cozy comforter and reassured myself over and over that it was that very same gentlemanly behavior that had prevented Matt from even trying to give me a good night kiss.

I reflected briefly on Matt's remarks regarding his previous relationship. I couldn't picture Matt jealous. . . .

"Like me, Matt," I whispered out loud as I drifted off to sleep. "I wouldn't make you jealous."

As usual, Dad was up early the next morning. He entered my room serenading me with "Oh, What A Beautiful Morning," just a shade or two off key. I pulled the blankets over my head but I was outnumbered. Cookie readily joined in on Dad's festive mood by jumping on my bed and nuzzling her way up under the covers, drenching me with sloppy kisses.

A born early riser, Dad can't understand my preference to "waste away" the morning hours of the day by sleeping late. He usually gives in on Saturday mornings, but come Sunday, our traditional day for family activities, he rouses me with his terrible singing.

After a shower and some hot tea, I began to feel human again. I thought about how if Mom were still alive, she'd have been in the kitchen already, preparing fried chicken for a picnic lunch. Instead, Dad and I planned to stop at the ski resort's Soup Kitchen and partake of some homemade soup and fresh bread.

Dad, Cookie, and I piled into the Bronco and headed south on the Seward Highway, along Turnagain Arm. I never get tired of the story of how Captain Cook sailed up the muddy inlet waters, searching for the legendary Inland Passage, only to discover that he had to turn again when he reached the arm's dead end.

Dad stopped at a turnout along the highway so we could climb around on some of the huge boulders that formed a barricade between the highway and the salt water. Like a sure-footed goat, Cookie ran on ahead of us. Whenever she decided that Dad and I had lagged too far behind, she'd tear back across the rocks to see what was taking us so long.

I was surprised to see that Cookie didn't really notice Cherub's absence, or at least, she didn't seem to mind. She was probably too busy soaking up all the extra attention Dad and I were giving her.

Thinking of Cherub, wondering how he was getting along at Dr. Hill's, and worrying that he might think we'd deserted him, the fears that had plagued me since Cherub's departure resurfaced. Dad had been purposefully cheerful all morning. So I hesitated before bringing up the subject, but I had to know. As Dad and I walked back up to the Bronco, I asked: "Dad, do you think Cherub will have to be put to sleep?"

I watched Dad's face, intent on picking up any nonverbal clues about the truth. His expression of surprise, then of sorrow, almost made me sorry I'd brought it up, after all.

"Honey, I honestly don't know. But, I'm afraid it's a possibility."

Strangely enough, I took in his words without breaking down in tears, my usual manner of handling heart-wrenching news. Although I felt an immeasurable sadness at the prospective loss of Cherub, at least Dad had been honest with me. We were facing tough, emotional times again, but we were facing them openly and together. So I tried my best to match Dad's strength and courage.

"Dad, I didn't mean to bum out our day. I guess I just needed to hear it said out loud, outside my own head. It's really a kind of relief to face up to the facts."

He smiled and said, "I understand completely, honey."

An hour later, we reached Portage Glacier. There's a road that goes all the way up and although Dad and I have made the trip at least a dozen times, each time the glacier looks different from before.

This time, the small glacier-fed lake was filled with all sizes of the floating jagged islands of blue ice. The glacier itself sat at the far side of the lake, tall and proud, an immense wall of compressed ice.

I tried to take some pictures of Dad and Cookie in front of the glacier, but a strong, cold wind kept blowing my hair in front of the camera lens. I finally gave up as it was obvious that the wind wouldn't. Dense gray clouds soon filled the sky and it wasn't long before we were running for the shelter of the Bronco.

By the time we finished our hot mugs of stewlike soup at the nearby ski resort, the rain was belting down. We ran across the parking lot but still got soaked. I fed Cookie a couple of sandwich scraps I'd saved for her and then we headed home.

The click-clack rhythm of the windshield wipers nearly put me to sleep. Half-awake, half-asleep, I began to dream of Matt. I saw the two of us together, dancing, gazing lovingly into each other's eyes. Would my dream ever come true? At least I was much closer to it than I'd ever have believed possible.

I became anxious to get back home in case Matt decided to call me again. About ten miles from town, we finally reached the edge of the springtime squall. A magnificent double rainbow appeared out over the water, each color sharply distinct from its neighboring hue. One end of the rainbow disappeared into the inlet waters, while the other end, the one with the pot of gold, landed somewhere in downtown Anchorage.

Something inside told me that the rainbow was a sign, an omen of good luck, for Matt and me. For surely, if I followed the rainbow to its end, it would lead me straight to Matt, the boy of my heart's desire.

10

Unfortunately, Sunday evening was disappointingly uneventful, meaning that Matt didn't call.

Well, what had I expected? After all, all that really had happened between us was a chance encounter at the lake and the sharing of a movie Matt hadn't wanted to attend alone. I knew from previous experience that boys found me easy to talk to, probably because about all I do is sit and listen, rarely contributing anything interesting to the conversation.

Finally admitting to myself that it was too late to hope Matt might still call, I phoned Bren to fill her in on the previous day's minor miracles. Even minor miracles only come around every century or so, I reminded myself, trying to dash any lingering unrealistic expectations.

"I was just about to call you," Bren told me. "Well, hurry up, Williams, spill it!"

Even though I was bursting to tell someone all about Matt, I wasn't sure how much of my true feelings I was ready to reveal. But the minute I heard her voice, I remembered that Bren and I had always been able to share everything, no matter how embarrassed or frightened we might feel.

Never adept at the fine art of beating around the bush, now that my mind was made up to reveal all, I simply blurted out, "Bren, I think I'm in love."

"What?"

Just as I'd expected, Bren sounded thoroughly shocked. Although it was nothing unusual before Randy had come along for Bren to announce her love for a different boy every week, I'd never once laid such a claim on any boy.

"You heard me. I'm totally flipped-out over Matt. Only problem is, I think he just likes me as a friend."

"OK, now, let's back up a minute and start from the beginning. I have the feeling I missed out on a few episodes."

So I began with the day I ran into Matt and Carol, this time telling her the whole story—about how I'd become entranced from the moment Matt laid his baby blues upon my feeble form. I went on in explicit detail about my afternoon with him at the lake, his surprise call that evening, and how comfortable I'd felt sharing memories of our old hometown.

"All of this sounds very promising. I think it's wonderful that Cupid's arrows have finally pierced your heart of steel. So why all the pessimism?"

"Because I think Matt's heart's already been pierced by Carol. She reminds him of his old girl friend," I told her glumly. "He'd already planned to take her to the Spring Dance, you know."

"You heard Mrs. MacDonald; none of us will have time for a date that night. Besides, you've already proven you're at least an even match for Carol. You got on the Board, didn't you? I say we go after him!"

"We? Bren, don't you dare breathe a word about this to him or any-body!"

"You know what I mean. With my boy know-how and your dedication to getting your man, you and he will be walking arm in arm in time for your birthday party."

I didn't reply. I wished I had my friend's confidence.

"How was your trip to Portage?" she asked, correctly sensing that it was time to let the subject of Matt rest for a while.

"Uneventful. It seemed strange without Cherub around. I'm worried about how Dad will handle it if . . . ." I did my best to explain to Bren why I thought Dad would suffer the most if we lost Cherub. Then another thought came to me.

"You know, Bren, this may sound funny, coming from his own daughter," I continued, "but don't you think Dad should have started seeing other women by now? I mean, it's been more than two years since Mom died."

"He's never had a single date since you guys moved here?" she asked with surprise. "I thought women would be pounding down his door. He's so good-looking, for an older man."

"You're talking about my dad?"

"You bet. A lot of women go crazy over that salt-and-pepper professorial look of his."

I tried to consider Dad in this new light, as the object of someone's romantic desire. The only way I could imagine it was to transfer the way I'd begun to feel about Matt to some imaginary woman who might someday have those kinds of feelings for Dad.

Suddenly Bren exclaimed, "I've got it! Mrs. Sutherlin."

"What? My speech teacher?" I said, shocked by Bren's suggestion. "She's married!"

"No, she's not. I know she never lets on otherwise, but she's a widow. Her husband died a long time ago. Since your dad and she are both teachers, they'd probably get along great."

Actually, the idea of Dad and Mrs. Sutherlin together was surprisingly appealing. In her office Friday afternoon, I'd felt the possibility of a special closeness developing between Mrs. Sutherlin and myself.

"I think you're right, Bren. And I know just the way to fix them up without their realizing it. I'd forgotten all about it, but Mrs. Sutherlin asked me to try to drum up additional chaperones for the Spring Dance. I'll volunteer Dad's services, then they'll meet at the dance. I'll make sure they get introduced; he's already heard about her from me. He's bound to ask her to dance at least once and from then on . . . who knows?"

Bren and I were still giggling over our conspiracy when Dad hollered up at me that he had a pot of hot chocolate all ready if there were anyone interested.

"Coming, Dad," I shouted back. "Gotta go, Bren. The perfect oppor-tunity just arose."

"OK, Ms. Matchmaker. Just don't forget we've got some work to do on *your* love life, as well."

"Don't worry," I told her. *"Him* I can't forget." *Be honest*, I thought to myself as we hung up, *you not only can't forget Matt, you really don't want to.*

"You *do* plan to come to the school dance next Saturday night?" I asked Dad as I handed him a steaming cup of chocolate. "Lend me some moral support?"

"You mean I have to submit myself to that ear-deafening music if I want to see my little girl perform in her star role?"

"Come on, Dad. I'll buy you some earplugs," I offered.

"Of course I'll be there, honey. Wouldn't miss it for the world."

"Thanks, Dad." Then, very casually, as though I'd just thought of it, I asked, "Say, since you'll be there anyway, how about helping Mrs. Sutherlin out? She's head of the chaperone committee and she told me she's having trouble lining up enough volunteers."

He eyed me suspiciously, then smiled and said, "Well, I suppose it wouldn't hurt to make myself useful for a change. But, don't forget the earplugs," he teased.

The next afternoon, Bren offered to drive me downtown to Farland's to begin my five-day crash modeling course.

"Thanks, Bren. Do you have time to stick around a while, just in case I need some moral support?" I asked her.

She said it would be no problem, and, boy, was I glad, because as it turned out, I needed all the help I could get.

My walk was wrong, I held my right shoulder higher than my left, and I couldn't make the end-of-ramp turn without stumbling. Long after Carol had graduated to Cosmetic Applications, I was still working on the basics.

It began to appear that my new career wouldn't last a day. I think Mrs. MacDonald and I were both on the verge of giving up when Bren interrupted, asking Mrs. MacDonald if she might have a few minutes with me. Mrs. MacDonald gave Bren a grateful smile and left us alone.

"Listen, Maggie, you're trying too hard," lectured Bren. "You've got the knack, you're just not as well-practiced as Carol. You've got to forget your self-consciousness and work at projecting an air of confidence."

For some reason, Bren's words made me remember the Maggie who'd stared back at me from the bathroom mirror Saturday afternoon—the older, more confident-looking Maggie, who'd later summoned enough self-assurance and poise to speak intelligible words in the presence of the boy of her dreams. I decided to give myself one more chance.

As I walked down the modeling ramp, I hung onto Bren's words, feeling secure in the knowledge that once I set my mind to it, I could do anything.

Luckily, I didn't notice that Mrs. MacDonald had reentered the room until after I'd reached the end of the ramp and performed an exquisite turn.

"Marvelous!" she cried. "I knew you had it in you."

The congratulations felt good, and what's more, I could tell—the way you know once you finally stay up on a bicycle—that I had the proper movement and carriage of my body for keeps, that there was no reason to fear losing it.

So for Mrs. MacDonald's benefit, I sashayed up and down the aisle several more times, then asked, "May I move on to Cosmetics now?"

Mrs. MacDonald and Bren both laughed at my eagerness. Then Mrs. MacDonald motioned me to follow her.

The lady from Cosmetics draped a couple of dozen different lengths of fabric across my neck, pointing out how some colors brightened and enhanced my appearance, while others made my skin look drab and washed out. After she'd chosen make-up colors that enhanced the best tones in my skin, she instructed me extensively on make-up application.

This time, because I now understood the "whys" behind the various highlighting and shadow-making procedures, I came much closer to reproducing the "model-look" on my own.

Just when I figured I was probably finished for the day, Mrs. Mac-Donald showed up to whisk me off to be measured and fitted by the in-store seamstress. After she'd pronounced me a perfect Petite size three, Mrs. MacDonald accompanied me to the new Petite Department where she helped me select my official Farland's Fashion Board outfit from the stock that had just arrived.

Deciding on aqua as my basic spring-summer color, we chose a full, softly pleated cotton skirt, with muted vertical bands of aqua, pale peach, and off-white. We matched it up with a hand-knit aqua cardigan since in Alaska, sweaters are in season all year long. Then we chose shoes and accessories to complement the outfit.

When I finally arrived home, just in time for a late dinner, my mind was spinning from all the colors, fashions, and instructions. The rest of the week seemed to buzz by, an indistinguishable blur of classes both at school and at Farland's.

Cherub did come home on Monday, as Dad had promised. I realized that I hadn't completely believed him and vowed to myself that in the future, I'd give more credit for treating me as an adult.

Even though I wasn't around much that week, I did notice that the pain in Cherub's joints was still there. If anything, it seemed to be getting worse.

Dr. Hill had prescribed a powerful painkiller to relieve Cherub's discomfort. This time, I'd rather Dad hadn't been so truthful with me. He explained that this medicine was a last resort for Cherub. If it didn't work, we had only three remaining choices.

Our first option was simply to do nothing. But who could stand to watch an animal they loved in continual pain? Secondly, we could allow Dr. Hill to attempt a surgical repair of the joints, a proposition that was painful, risky, and not a certain cure. Dad didn't say as much, but I gathered that this second option was also way above our budget. The last choice available to us was to have Dr. Hill put Cherub out of his misery, quickly, painlessly. A choice I didn't want to think about.

So I was thankful for the diversion my new position provided all week, except that it left me with no time for Matt. My only consolation was that at least I knew he wasn't spending it with Carol, since she, too, was busy attending modeling classes every day.

On Thursday night, Dad asked me where I wanted to go for my birthday dinner the following evening. Naturally I chose Simon & Seafort's, because the restaurant has such an outrageous view of the sun setting out over Cook Inlet, and I've always been a nut for gorgeous sunsets!

So when the hostess escorted us to a window table Friday evening, I knew Dad had called ahead to prearrange the special seating. We worked our way through deep-fried zucchini, spinach and bacon salad, prime rib, and lobster, and were waiting for the chocolate mousse when Dad reached into his pocket and pulled out a small gift-wrapped box.

"Mom wanted me to give this to you when you graduated, but I think you've shown such an adult sense of responsibility that you deserve to have it a little early."

Dad's so sweet and funny and always so official sounding. You'd think this was an awards banquet instead of a birthday party. Still, I wondered what could be in the box.

I didn't waste any time finding out. Inside the silver wrapping paper I discovered a jewelry case. Inside the case lay my mother's pink pearl necklace.

"Dad! Mom's necklace! Oh, thank you, it's gorgeous."

I wondered if Dad knew that I'd been sneaking peeks into the box of her belongings that he kept in his bedroom closet. Sometimes, when I missed her especially badly, I'd secretly go through her keepsakes one by one. I'd always been particularly enthralled by the necklace I now held in my hands.

Dad got up and came around to do the clasp for me. The pearls felt smooth, cool, and silky against my neck. I thought I detected just the faintest aroma of my mother's favorite scent.

"I'll cherish the necklace forever and ever," I told Dad.

My dessert came along shortly thereafter, together with a candle and a song. Everybody around us joined in with the waiter and waitress to sing me a happy birthday. I made my wish—naturally it was centered on Matt—and blew out the candle. We watched the sunset and then Dad asked for the bill. It was a perfect evening.

I went to bed as soon as we got home; I would be facing a big day the next morning. Mrs. MacDonald had scheduled our dress rehearsal from 9:00 to 12:00; then of course the real thing was that evening.

I was dying of curiosity as to whether anything might develop between Dad and Mrs. Sutherlin. And even though I was still feeling pessimistic about my chances with Matt, I couldn't help dreaming about the possibility of seeing him under circumstances more romantic than at school.

11

My first thoughts upon awakening the next morning weren't about my birthday, my mother's pearls, or even Matt. All I could think of was: Today's the day I become a real model!

I was anxious to see the outfits Mrs. MacDonald had picked out; each girl got to model an outfit from three categories—school wear, at-play wear, and dressy wear—to coincide with the band's three breaks.

When Bren and I arrived, Mrs. MacDonald stood beside a long, free-standing clothing rack, reading names from her clipboard and distributing the outfits. The category with the most variety was the at-play clothing; it included tennis outfits, jogging attire, designer jeans, shorts sets, and, of course, bathing suits. (We have a lot of indoor pools up here.) Bren and I gave each other sidelong smirks as Mrs. MacDonald handed Carol a skimpy-looking bikini.

My first score was an electric-blue chamois jump suit. It was belted at the waist, with narrow military-style tabs across the padded shoulders, and three-quarter length, roll-up sleeves.

I tried on the jump suit, along with the accessories that were all numbered in a big box. For an older woman, Mrs. MacDonald had an excellent sense of style. She'd matched my outfit with low-heeled, cherry-colored pumps, choker-length twisted beads, and earrings to match. A cherry-and-blue-striped cardigan thrown casually over my shoulder completed my at-school outfit.

Bren walked up behind me as I was studying myself in the mirror.

"You look smashing in that outfit, Maggie. That color of blue really makes your eyes stand out."

I looked closer and saw that she was right; my normally rather pale blue eyes appeared a brilliant blue. Too bad the effect wouldn't be visible from the audience; naturally I thought of the one person I'd like to have close enough to notice.

Then Mrs. MacDonald called out Bren's name and handed her a stunning red-chiffon creation that looked as though it were designed for a prom queen.

My dressy outfit turned out to be a two-piece linen suit with a matching hat that had a little veil that came down over my eyes. The outfit looked crisp and sophisticated, all in navy and white.

The third outfit I was assigned to model was a bright-pink shorts set, complete with sunglasses and sandals. Mrs. MacDonald suggested I pull my long hair up into a side ponytail to complete the casual look.

After everyone had all the pieces of their outfits together, we took a short break while Mr. Gorman, our school janitor, along with several student volunteers, finished transforming our lunchroom into an auditorium.

Some makeshift dressing rooms had been jury-rigged from the free-standing room dividers that usually stood in the study hall. An emergency call to Farland's brought additional mirrors, and a couple of lunch tables served as our dressing tables.

"I hadn't realized this would be such a production," I overheard Mrs. MacDonald mumble to herself.

But at last Mr. Gorman got the intercom system to work without the ear-shattering hum and Mrs. MacDonald took her place at the podium to recite the show commentary.

Since all of the girls except Carol and me were already well-experienced in the standard show procedure, our rehearsal was flowing quite smoothly when at last I heard my cue and made ready to enter stage right. What happened instead is that I not only didn't make it out on cue, I didn't make it out at all.

"Introducing Farland's new Petite line of Junior clothing, Maggie Williams is ready to parachute into spring wearing this electric-blue jump suit by Esprit," announced Mrs. MacDonald with a voice full of charm and sophistication.

I tossed the cardigan over my shoulder in imitation of the casual, aloof looks I'd seen on models in fashion magazines. But as I began to walk toward the stage area, I felt a gentle tug from behind me.

Concentrating on my timing, I kept walking, but then there came an even firmer resistance to my forward motion. Expecting to see Bren behind me, pulling at my sweater to tease me, I gave a sharp tug and then turned to face a room divider about to flatten me.

I tried to leap out of the way but, unaccustomed even to low heels, I tripped over my own feet. I felt my right foot scrunch into an abnormal position and my toes wrenched upward.

When everything quit falling, Bren was the first one beside me.

"Maggie, are you OK?" she asked.

"I might have twisted something, my foot hurts a little."

Then, remembering I had to walk on that foot to be able to participate in the show that evening, I quickly added, "But, I'm sure it'll be fine in a minute."

Carol and Mrs. MacDonald were the next to arrive. "What happened, Maggie?" Mrs. MacDonald asked me sympathetically.

Before I could get the first word out, Carol volunteered, "I saw everything! Maggie's sweater got caught on the corner of the room divider; from then on, it was just like watching dominoes fall." She smiled, either proud of her simile or exceptionally pleased by my disgraceful display.

Of course, I felt like a perfect idiot. It was the first day of my modeling lessons all over again, only worse, because this was the real thing. I doubted I'd ever win back Mrs. MacDonald's respect.

I sat there too dumbstruck to say a word, I just knew Mrs. MacDonald's next words would be to ask me to leave.

"OK, now," announced Mrs. MacDonald, "let's work together and get this set orderly again."

Mr. Gorman and his three helpers—Harold Brenski, Leonard Johnson, and Billy Sanders—came over to set the room divider upright again. This time they stabilized it with additional braces.

Bren helped me up and brushed me off. At least the outfit wasn't torn or dirty. I looked at Mrs. MacDonald and fought back the tears.

"Are you sure you're OK?" she asked kindly. When I nodded my head, she said, "All right then, birthday girl, let's do take two. Come on, everybody!"

She gave me a warm smile and then headed for the podium. I walked barefoot back to the dressing room—my right foot throbbed slightly—and tried not to think about how quickly this story would get spread around Ridgeway.

At least Mrs. MacDonald had been understanding and didn't seem to mind giving me another chance. I guessed she was getting used to it by now.

When my next cue came, my appearance on stage was timed just right and I traveled down the modeling ramp in what seemed to me perfect form, even though the little toe on my right foot had begun to feel as if it were on fire.

We completed the final sets with minimal delays. As we finished putting our outfits away, Mrs. MacDonald called for our attention.

"Would everyone please meet me down here by the front doors before leaving?"

When we'd all gathered around, she told us that she wanted everyone to return by seven o'clock, an hour before the dance was scheduled to begin. Someone asked her if we would be allowed to dance between sets and she said she didn't mind as long as everyone remained responsible enough to be ready on time.

"I have one other announcement to make and then you're all free for the afternoon—and I suggest that if it's at all possible, everyone should get some beauty rest before tonight's show."

Then she turned and looked expectantly toward the front doors. A bakery truck pulled up and a man in white pants and shirt ran up to the door with a large white box in his hands.

"This isn't quite how I'd planned it," she said apologetically. "Please turn around, Maggie."

I heard some rustling and the striking of matches and then the room erupted in "Happy Birthday to You," and I turned to see a beautiful rose-covered cake with 16 flaming candles.

This time I couldn't hold back the tears.

12

We all enjoyed some birthday cake and left the school grounds by noon. That meant there was another seven hours to kill before we had to be back for the show.

The sky was a deep, clear blue and the mountains still wore white caps of snow as Bren and I climbed in Betsy. Bren pointed toward the numerous small aircraft that dotted the sky.

"Maybe Matt's up there somewhere right now," she teased.

She must have been reading my mind because ever since that day at the lake, whenever I saw a small plane, it made me think of Matt. Of course, it didn't really take much to make me think of Matt. He loved flying so much, I just knew he was a good and careful pilot.

"Maybe," I said, evasively.

"You're awfully tight-lipped this afternoon. You sure you're not still feeling bad over this morning's mishap?"

"Oh, well, maybe a little," I answered, not wanting to tell her that the real reason I was so quiet was that I was concentrating on not letting on about the pain in my little toe. "But, you're right, Matt could be up there. Actually, Bren, I'd rather you didn't even bring him up. It just makes me feel worse thinking about him, since I know there's no chance of anything's happening between us."

"Yeah? I think you're wrong," said Bren as she pulled up to my house.

She paused a minute, then added, "I can see I'm going to have to do some matchmaking of my own to get you and Matt together tonight."

"Brenda Jackson, you'd better not. I mean it!"

"But, Maggie, he'd make such a nice birthday present. . . ."

I gave her my evil-eye stare.

"OK, OK, just teasing."

"That's all it'd better be. Don't you dare go talking to him about me." Then, as though it were an afterthought, I asked, "Think he'll even be at the dance tonight?"

"Sure he will. Now you just calm down. Do what Mrs. MacDonald suggested and get a little rest this afternoon. I'll be back at a quarter to seven. Oh, almost forgot—happy birthday!"

Bren pulled a sack out from beneath her seat and handed it to me. Inside the sack from Farland's was a small assortment of cosmetics, along with a peach-colored box that I recognized immediately. Naturally, none of it was wrapped. Bren hates to wrap presents, she doesn't have the patience.

"Oh, Bren, thank you!"

The box contained my favorite perfume, a brand too expensive for me to purchase under normal circumstances. The cosmetics were ones that Sheri had recommended as supplemental to what I'd already purchased.

"Hope you like it all . . . hope you can figure out what to do with it," she kidded.

"Thanks a lot," I said. Actually, she was closer to the truth than I cared to admit.

I got out of Betsy and waved good-bye, then hesitated a few seconds before opening the front door.

I stood there realizing how, more and more, I'd begun to think of Cherub's illness as a permanent disability. I wondered what Dad was deciding to do about Cherub. What if Cherub weren't there when I opened the door?

But as I stepped inside the entryway, both puppies came running to greet me, Cherub with his slight limp, Cookie rambunctious as ever. I figured Dad would be in his office working; the puppies had probably been curled up under the desk against his feet, as they both had that "just-woke-up" look in their big golden-brown eyes.

"Hi, Dad. I'm home," I called from outside his office door, waiting for him to indicate whether it was a good or bad time to disrupt his work.

But since today was my birthday, I knew he'd give me first consideration. I remembered our wonderful dinner last night and the gift of my mother's pearls.

"Hi, sweetheart. How'd rehearsal go?"

"Not too smoothly, actually," I said as I entered his office. I quickly filled him in on my "accident."

"But it all turned out OK in the end, didn't it?"

"I guess so, except when I tripped, I fell on my foot."

His cheerful expression was replaced with one of parental concern.

"I thought I noticed a slight limp."

"You noticed? I didn't think it showed."

"Come over here and let me take a look."

I hobbled over to the couch where I could stretch out and let Dad examine my foot. He took my sock off and began maneuvering my foot up, down, and around in a circle. Satisfied that my ankle wasn't injured, he massaged my foot from heel to toe. When he got to my little toe, I let out a holler.

"Aha! Found something. Hang on a minute, let me have a better look at this poor little toe."

He manipulated it, more gently this time, and decided that it was just a strained muscle. He asked if I wanted a real doctor's opinion. It really didn't hurt *that* badly, and I knew a vote to see my doctor would have killed my chances to model that night. What a birthday that would be, sitting at home!

"You know, Maggie, you really should stay off that foot."

"Dad! I just can't miss tonight's performance. I'll lie down all afternoon, OK? Besides, you've got to go anyway, to chaperone, remember?"

He had that "I'm-not-so-sure-about-that" look on his face, so I kept right on talking, hoping he'd ease up if I got him sidetracked for a while.

"Which reminds me, Mrs. Sutherlin wanted me to ask you to be sure to look for her tonight." I wanted to make sure the two of them got together to give my matchmaking scheme a chance.

"Maggie," he said in a serious voice, "are you still having problems in her class?"

I could see the conversation was turning the wrong way so I told him quickly, "No, nothing like that. In fact, I'm doing really well in her class. Actually, I may have mentioned your research; I think she just wants to meet you and hear about it firsthand."

The key to Dad's heart is an expressed interest in his pet research project. I watched as he reconsidered.

"OK, we'll go. I don't imagine that three trips up and down the modeling ramp will kill you. But no fast dancing, promise?" My face fell. "I'm sorry, honey, I know it's your birthday."

"How about slow dances?" Naturally I was thinking of Matt. How could I get a chance to be with him if I couldn't even dance?

"It's against my better judgment, but since it's your birthday, OK. Just take it easy, Maggie."

After I'd promised to be careful, Dad told me to look on top of the hall table. I already knew what I'd find.

When Mom was alive, she always saved up all the mail and packages that arrived before my birthday. Dad had kept up the tradition.

Most of the mail I inspected was stamped with Oregon postmarks, but there was one from Florida that would be from my Aunt Nolan. I saved it for last since past experience told me it would be my favorite gift. And sure enough, it was a wonderfully soft flannel nightgown along with a pair of fuzzy house slippers. I smiled at Aunt Nolan's gifts; she was determined in her belief that inhabitants of Alaska were in perpetual danger of freezing to death.

Many of the cards had gifts of money in them. I planned to use that to improve my wardrobe just as soon as my Farland's discount went into effect. New clothes, the make-up and perfume from Bren—this was definitely going to be my year of self-improvement.

I collected my gifts and headed for Dad's office to show him what I'd gotten. He was already back to work at his desk so I made it brief. I wrestled around on the living room rug with the puppies for a while, then headed up the stairs to rest my foot, as I'd promised Dad. I figured I could use a nap anyway.

It was already almost two o'clock, so I set my alarm for four, in case I did happen to drift off. At first though, I just lay there, too nervous about the upcoming evening to fall asleep. So to take my mind off of all the things I might do wrong that night, I thought about Matt.

I gazed out my window and saw two small planes. I singled one out and pretended it held Matt and his uncle. I pictured Matt asking his uncle to point out the location of 44th and Birch—my house, of course. After that, I imagined Matt and me together, flying around the bright-blue sky, free as the sea gulls that also flew past my window.

The next thing I knew, Dad was shaking me, asking me if I didn't need to start getting ready. I grabbed the alarm clock beside me and read 5:30.

"The stupid alarm didn't go off," I complained.

"I'll bet the stupid alarm would work better if someone remembered to turn it on."

He was right. I'd forgotten. I thanked him for waking me and jumped up. I noticed my foot did feel better and made sure Dad knew it. He told me I still couldn't dance the fast dances.

I had planned on an afternoon of leisurely preparation for the special evening. I wanted to look my very best in case I saw Matt.

Instead I had to rush to get ready in time. The adrenalin started pumping the moment Dad woke me so that I ended up with a self-induced case of the jitters. Just what I didn't need on the night of my modeling debut.

At 6:45, as I paced the hallway waiting for Bren, it suddenly occurred to me to ask Dad what he planned to wear. When he replied that he really hadn't thought about it, I flew into a panic.

Dad is notorious for mismatching clothing in both color and style. He never seemed to have developed an eye for properly put-together attire.

So I rushed into his bedroom and laid his cashmere pullover, button-down striped shirt, wool slacks, and blue socks neatly on his unmade bed. I almost slipped up by not remembering to pick out his shoes as well. I found his dressy slip-ons and set them in plain sight beside the bed.

By the time Brenda arrived, ten minutes late, I was a nervous wreck, feeling my least beautiful and without a spark of self-confidence. The minute I saw her pulling in the driveway, I flew out the front door without giving anyone—Dad or the puppies—their good-bye hugs. I heard Dad call out "See you tonight" from behind the slammed door.

Only later did I discover that the afternoon's hecticness was but a warm-up for the disasters that would befall me on the evening of my 16th birthday.

13

Bren managed to diminish my composure even further by cutting 5 minutes off the usual 15-minute trip to Ridgeway High. We still arrived 10 minutes late to find the entire auditorium in pandemonium. From what I could see, the only thing ready was the decorations.

The Decoration Committee had performed a wondrous transformation on Ridgeway's normally dull lunchroom. Students from the Art Department had painted the butcher-papered walls with scenes reminiscent of French impressionist pastorals. Bright reds, greens, and yellows dominated the springtime atmosphere. The junior class, who was sponsoring the dance, had rented large potted plants—the size of small trees, actually—and scattered them around the dance floor for a gardenlike effect. In one corner of the room sat a scaled-down model of a brilliantly striped hot-air balloon, on loan from the show floor of a local car dealership. At the opposite end of the room, volunteers were setting up a refreshment table.

I spotted Harold Brenski up on the stage, helping out with the Blasters' elaborate sound system. He was giving orders to Leonard and Billy who are, if possible, even dorkier than Harold.

Behind Harold and his friends, a constant humming chatter came from the makeshift dressing room. A few teachers and chaperones had arrived early and they were congregating over by the refreshment table.

I thought it was too good to be true but Mrs. MacDonald hadn't shown up yet, so Bren and I were conveniently off the hook for our tardiness.

We joined the other girls and found most of them still checking to see that all of the accessories for each of their outfits were gathered together, to avoid any last-minute panic. The few girls who'd arrived early, as I'd planned to do, were already messing with their make-up or fussing with curling irons and hair spray.

Some commotion broke out at the far end of one of the make-up tables, momentarily drawing everyone's attention. Linda Babbles couldn't find the cerise scarf that was part of her first outfit. She was interrogating Karen Gatlin, who at rehearsal that morning had expressed a strong desire to own that scarf.

Dismissing the ensuing argument, I soon discovered that I had problems of my own. I couldn't find the shoes I'd been wearing that morning when I'd inadvertently torn the set apart. Apparently they'd gotten lost in the shuffle. I asked Bren about them, but she hadn't picked them up either.

Then I remembered that Harold, who always volunteered for off-beat and non-glamorous jobs like setting up the stage area for the school dance, had been present that morning. I'd been too preoccupied with the embarrassing situation and a painful little toe to notice, but I felt sure that Harold had probably helped Mr. Gorman pick up the mess I'd made.

For once grateful for Harold's proximity, I started across the stage to ask him about my shoes, but got waylaid by a member of the band.

"Hey, missy, where you runnin' to in such a hurry?" said a boy dressed in a spacey purple cowboy outfit as he stepped out in front of me.

He spoke with a real cute Southern accent and then I remembered that the Blasters were from Texas. I'd heard that several members had originally come to Alaska looking for high-paying jobs in the oil field. When the jobs didn't materialize, they took up where they'd left off in Texas, playing rock-and-roll for a living.

All of Ridgeway High was excited that the Blasters had agreed to perform at a lowly high school function . . . and at a reduced fee.

"I've got to ask that boy something," I said, pointing toward Harold. *As though it's any of your business*, I thought to myself. Still, another part of me tingled with excitement that a real live rocker was showing an interest in nobody-Maggie.

"He your boyfriend?" he asked in a derisive tone.

"No, he's not my boyfriend. I've lost the shoes to one of the outfits I'll be modeling tonight and he was at the dress rehearsal. I think he might have picked them up." I hoped he wouldn't think to inquire as to why Harold would have been picking up my shoes.

"Well, I'd be happy to assist you in your search. Let's try this direction." As he spoke, he took hold of my arm and moved to turn me in the opposite direction from Harold. Apparently he wasn't as worried as I was about getting ready in time.

"Sorry, I'm certain Harold will know where to find the shoes. Thanks, anyway."

I couldn't believe my own ears as I listened to myself turning him down. I pulled my arm free from his firm grip and continued on my way toward Harold.

At first, from the look of astonishment on his face, I was afraid he was going to get mad. But then he grinned and said, "Business first, huh? I like a woman who takes care of her business! OK, then, see you after the show." Then, as though it were an afterthought, he asked, "Say, what's your name, anyway?"

His superior manner was really turning me off. I hate people who are as stuck on themselves as this guy appeared to be. Even so, I didn't want to appear snooty, so I called my name back over my shoulder and kept going. Then I realized he hadn't even told me his name. He probably assumed that since he was such a star, I'd know it already.

When I reached Harold, he was concentrating on his job so hard that he didn't hear me walk up behind him. I spoke his name, which made him jump and let out a big holler.

"Maggie! What are you doing here? I mean, I'm sure glad to see you. You startled me, that's all. So—what's up?"

"*If* you'd let me get a word in edgewise," I said, giving him a friendly smile to show I wasn't making fun of him, "you'd find out that I came over to ask if you can remember what happened to the shoes I was wearing after I so gracefully pulled down the entire set this morning."

"As a matter of fact, I do," he told me with great pride.

"Oh, Harold, you're a lifesaver," I cried perhaps a bit too ecstatically. I saw his eyes light up and I suddenly realized that a boy like Harold might easily misconstrue my enthusiasm. I wasted no time explaining, "I mean, I'd just die if I messed up my own modeling debut."

"Oh, yeah, I know what you mean," he said, displaying considerably less eagerness.

"Well?"

He looked at me like "Well, what?" and then suddenly seemed to remember why I was standing there.

"Oh. Carol picked them up. Last I saw." Then he unceremoniously turned back to his work.

His answer only served to stroke the fires of my perturbed state of mind. I mumbled my thanks and steam-engined over to where I'd last seen Carol working meticulously on her make-up. Bren once told me that Carol spent at least 30 minutes every day just doing her make-up.

When I found her, she'd progressed to doing her hair. I was mad enough to take care of the job for her by pulling out every last strand.

"Carol!"

I waited for her to turn toward me with her usual "above-thee" expression plastered on her face. Instead I saw nothing but a nervous, frightened girl, and for a minute forgot about my anger.

"Carol," I said again, "what's the matter?"

But the vulnerability I'd read on her face disappeared even as I spoke and her normal, masklike expression returned.

"Nothing. What's the matter with you?"

"Harold says you took my red heels."

"I didn't 'take' them; I had them in safekeeping. You went stumbling off with Bren and Mrs. MacDonald so I picked them up. I was planning to bring them over to you as soon as I'd finished my hair, OK? They're right there," she said, pointing at her bag under the table.

I said "thank you" and reached down for my shoes, feeling a little contrite after nearly accusing Carol of stealing them. Although still unsure as to whether she were telling me the truth, I wanted to give her the benefit of doubt. But Carol's next words made her true motives only too clear.

"And by the way, Maggie. You might as well forget about Matt Brennan. I know you were with him at the Super Duper Saturday night. He called me first, you know. My mother took the message. Unfortunately I already *had* a date. I'm not used to last-minute requests for a date."

Carol's revelation left me so tongue-tied from shock that I simply stared at her for a couple of seconds and then, without saying a single word, I spun around and fled from her sight.

The meaning of her words hit me like a cement truck. The only reason Matt had asked me for a date was because he couldn't get the girl he'd really wanted on such short notice. No wonder he had been so apologetic about calling me at the last minute. He'd probably just gotten off the phone from trying Carol.

I ran, even though my little toe was killing me, for the privacy of the girls' restroom. Hiding out in a stall, my tears fell as I suffered alone the sting of Carol's words.

14

Somehow I managed to regain enough self-composure to finish getting ready for the first modeling set with time left over to check out the beginning of the dance. Even though I knew I'd be too embarrassed even to consider telling Bren how badly I'd been duped, I went looking for her.

How could Matt have been so heartless? I asked myself as I headed for the dance floor. On the other hand, what right did I have to accuse him? It wasn't as though he'd puposefully deceived me—I was simply his second choice.

The lights were dimmed as Mr. Irving unlocked the door in front of the ticket table. There was already a crowd of kids lined up to get inside.

As my eyes adjusted to the darkly lit room, I looked around for Dad first. When I didn't see him anywhere, I decided he was probably going to be late.

I spotted Mrs. Sutherlin right away though. She was busy helping at the ticket table, greeting and conversing with the kids as they came in the door. I'd never seen her in anything besides street clothes and tonight she was all dressed up. She'd even done her hair differently and I thought she looked especially pretty.

Then I saw Dad at the front door, trying to squeeze past the line of students. Mrs. Sutherlin spoke to him as soon as he got inside. They shook hands, conversed back and forth for a minute, and then both of them burst out laughing. It looked as though I wouldn't have to worry about Dad.

So then I joined Bren who was standing with a group of kids in a large circle up at the very front of the dance floor, as close to the stage area as possible. The Blasters were busy tuning their instruments, making all kinds of other-worldly noises. There were four of them: a drummer, pianist, bass guitarist, and the lead singer, who also played guitar. The latter was the boy with the big ego who'd promised to look for me after the dance.

"Hello, out there!" shouted the singer—I still didn't know his name. What I did know was that the more I watched him strut around the stage, as though all the girls were just dying to touch him, the less I cared.

The crowd responded with some loud cheering, hoots, and whistles. "Thanks!" said Mr. Conceited. "We're happy to see you, too. We call ourselves the Blasters. . . ." More cheering and hooting. "And we've come here tonight to help Ridgeway High celebrate the arrival of spring. A time when a young man's fancy turns to . . . baseball?" (A few cheers from the crowd.) ". . . fishing?" (A few more cheers from the crowd.) ". . . wait a minute, I've got it . . . LOVE!!!" (A big roar of approval from the crowd.) "That's right! SO, wadda ya say? Let's dance!"

As he spoke the last two words, he threw his raised arm down and the music started with a crash of the drummer's cymbals.

Kids started pairing off immediately. Naturally, to get the crowd moving, the band's first song was some fast-paced rock-and-roll.

Just as I was about to vacate the area—after all, I couldn't dance anyway—who should appear from out of nowhere but Matt. All of a sudden, there he was, standing between Carol and me, asking, "Would you like to dance?"

The pit of my stomach turned over as all of my previous jealousies toward Carol flared to the surface. Preferring not to witness her acceptance, I kept my back turned.

But then I heard his voice again, saying, "Maggie?" I turned in wonderment—was he asking me?

"Oh . . . hi, Matt. Did you want something?" I asked him nonchalantly, stalling by instinct rather than guile.

"Yes, I did," he said. "Would you like to dance?"

By now, our circle of kids had thinned out considerably. I stood there
in a half-daze for I don't know how long, until I felt a nearby dancer
bump into me. Just as it occurred to me to answer yes, I remembered the
promise I'd made to my dad. I knew I had to tell Matt no, when my whole
self longed to say yes, yes, yes!

"Thanks very much," I shouted over the loud music, "but . . . I can't
right now. Can I have a rain check?" I added foolishly.

"What?" he asked. "Sounds like you said no."

Even though there was some poetic justice in my turning Matt down, I
ached to explain the predicament I was in because of my stupid toe. But
the only way to communicate over the deafening music was to shout—
not exactly the most ideal circumstances for a lengthy, not to mention
secret, explanation. Carol and a few others were still standing right next
to me. If they overheard me telling Matt that I couldn't dance because I'd
injured my foot, there was no question in my mind that one of them,
probably Carol, would report it to Mrs. MacDonald. I even thought
about forgetting my promise to Dad just this once.

In the split second it took for me to consider all these possibilities,
Carol was obviously doing some quick thinking of her own.

"I'd love to dance, Matt," purred Carol. "If *you* don't take me, I might
not get to dance at all," she pouted cutely, knowing very well what an
absurd suggestion she was making.

I couldn't see Matt's expression as he turned from me to face Carol.
Was he smiling at her in the same concerned, caring manner as he'd
smiled at me? Total confusion enveloped me. Why had Matt asked *me*
first when Carol had been standing in plain sight right beside me? I could
hardly bear to watch as he offered his arm and led her a few yards away to a
small opening among the dancers.

I stood there watching them dance, trying to console myself as well as I
could. At least it wasn't a slow dance they were sharing. And when a slow

dance did come up, well, then I might still have a chance with Matt. That is, if he weren't already so turned off by my initial rejection or if Carol didn't keep him tethered to her for the rest of the evening.

Since Bren was off somewhere with Randy and I desperately needed some moral support, I looked around for Dad. When I finally spotted him, I had to laugh. He was standing in the far corner of the room, behind the refreshment table partition, doing everything short of actually covering his ears to escape the Blasters' high-volume music.

"Hi, Dad," I shouted when I got near enough. When he looked my way, I saw his face light up. I thought of how great it is to be considered that special by at least one person in this world, even if it's your own dad.

We were waiting for the song to end so we'd be able to talk to each other without screaming, but the band fooled us by going right into another song. As I listened, the tempo slowed and I could see that Carol and Matt were still dancing together. Only now it was a slow dance.

"Hi, honey, how's your little toe doing?" he asked.

"Feels pretty good. I'm sure I could dance on it just fine," I complained.

"I'm sure you could, too, but that doesn't mean I'm going to let you." Parents can be so unrelenting.

We visited for a few more minutes until the Blasters turned up their volume again. Then I told Dad I needed to go and get ready; actually I still had plenty of time, but I was so confused by Matt's actions and bummed about missing my chance to dance with him—not to mention being totally nerved out about my imminent performance—that I needed to be alone. I excused myself and headed backstage.

I'd only been sitting at the dressing table for a couple of songs when Bren showed up. Apparently she wasn't so preoccupied with Randy that she didn't notice my absence.

"I can't believe it! Sissie Hornell told me that Matt asked you to dance and you turned him down flat. Is that true, Maggie?"

"I'm afraid so."

"Why? It was the perfect chance. I told you he'd notice you."

"You don't have to rub it in. I feel miserable enough," I told her. "Promise to keep a secret?"

"Of course, scout's honor."

"When I fell this morning, I pulled a muscle in my little toe. It's not really bad as long as I walk carefully. But, honest-injun me, I had to go and tell Dad about it. He made me promise no fast dancing tonight. Real great, right? Can't dance on my own birthday with the only boy I ever really wanted to dance with."

"Oh, Maggie, I'm sorry. But why didn't you at least explain this to Matt?"

"And take the chance that Carol would overhear and tell Mrs. Mac-Donald? She'd probably make me drop out of tonight's program."

"I doubt even Carol would stoop that low."

"You do, huh? Well, guess what Ms. Upperclasswoman just couldn't wait to tell me?"

I hadn't planned on it, but I couldn't pass up the opportunity to show Bren just how mean Carol could be. After I'd repeated what Carol had told me, as well as the part about her having my shoes, Bren said, "She could be lying about his calling her, you know."

Suddenly my heart sprouted wings. Why hadn't I thought of that? It was a real possibility. I fully believed Carol capable of spite at almost any cost. It would have been an easy thing for her to find out that we'd been at the Super Duper; if she were lying, it would explain why Matt had asked me to dance first.

Maybe, just maybe, I *was* the one he wanted.

But I didn't have time to consider the intricacies of the jumbled-up situation any longer as it was suddenly time for me to line up for our first modeling set.

In just a few minutes, I'd have to walk onstage in front of hundreds of my classmates. A shiver of fear and excitement crept up my spine. Would I meaure up? Or would I look as stiff and scared as I felt?

15

"Ladies and gentlemen, welcome to Farland's Spring Fashion Show. Tonight's presentation will take place in three segments. Our program begins with outfits designed to help you step down the school halls in springtime style."

Linda Babbles was first in line. Boy, was I thankful I didn't have that position. My place was fifth, just ahead of Carol, so I would be the first new girl to go onstage. This fact gave me a certain degree of secret satisfaction; it was as though, for once anyway, I was one up on Carol.

"Making her debut as one of the new members on our Fashion Board, Maggie Williams wears this year's favorite jump suit. . . ."

Right on cue, I made my way into view of what seemed like a million faces. Just as I reached center stage, a blinding spotlight flashed across my body, then fixed itself on me.

What happened next was that I tried to take a step forward but discovered myself paralyzed, immobilized by a massive case of stage fright.

So I concentrated on blacking out everything and everyone around me, as Mrs. Sutherlin had taught me to do. I added to that the measured breathing technique and magically, my legs began to work again.

The entire episode lasted less than a minute, Dad told me later that he'd thought I was just striking a pose like other models he'd seen.

I reached the end of the ramp and executed a smooth turn, making the return trip without a flaw.

Still focused on blanking out everything but my performance, I didn't realize that Mrs. MacDonald's commentary was no longer part of the show as we'd rehearsed it until I was almost offstage.

"Maggie, would you please step over here to the microphone for a minute?"

I was scared to death she'd ask me a question and then I'd have to speak into that thing. When I thought about everybody who was out there watching me, I really began to work up a sweat. It wasn't just the crowd of kids that frightened me, although that was bad enough, but the special people, like Dad and Mrs. Sutherlin. And Matt.

I walked toward Mrs. MacDonald, trying to hide the terror that was devouring me on the inside. It wasn't working. Red-hot embarrassment flooded my face.

"Please excuse Maggie's confusion, everybody. This wasn't in tonight's program." She turned and gave me a confidence-inspiring smile, then said, "Our other new model, Carol Conners, wears this season's version of the school-girl jumper. . . ."

On Carol's return trip up the ramp, Mrs. MacDonald motioned her over to the podium also, so that the two of us stood dwarf-like on either side of the statuesque Mrs. MacDonald.

"I wanted to interrupt tonight's show for just a minute to extend officially a warm welcome to Maggie and Carol. Our two new models will be representing Farland's Junior Petite line of clothing, for all you pretty little girls under 5'2"."

Then she started up a round of applause. Carol and I stood there with parade-queen smiles pasted ear to ear. As the clapping died down, I took that as our cue to exit and Carol followed.

Safely behind the stage sceens, I said to Carol, "Oh, that was so embarrassing. Weren't you surprised?"

"I was surprised, but I didn't think it was all that embarrassing. As a matter of fact, I thought it was kind of fun standing up there, looking out at everybody."

"Yes," I answered, "but all those everybodies were staring back at just us three bodies, mostly at yours and mine."

Carol just shrugged her shoulders, as if to say, "So what?" If I'd had any doubts, I knew then that there was definitely a basic difference in Carol's and my character make-up.

I got changed and back out to the dance floor just as the Blasters roared onstage. This time, the singer went through a medley of introductions, so that I finally found out that his name was Tom. Tom faced the audience, and with a deep voice that he probably thought sounded smooth and intimate, he leaned down really close to the microphone and said:

"We're going to start this set off with a song for all you springtime lovers. This one's called 'Heartbeat'; I wrote it myself."

As if we cared.

As the dancers paired off, I suddenly felt rather conspicuous standing all alone. So I began to scrutinize the crowd for a tall, dark-haired boy with bright-blue eyes, as it turned out that "Heartbeat" was a slow song.

Just as I decided to head for the crowd of kids gathered around the refreshment table, I felt someone tap me on my left shoulder. I whirled around, but no one was there. Deep, musical laughter came from my right side though, telling me I'd just fallen for one of the oldest tricks around. I turned the other way to see who was playing games with me.

It was Matt!

"Last chance, Maggie," he warned. "Would you please dance with this poor, friendless new kid?"

Naturally I couldn't speak a word. I did manage an enthusiastic nod and an ear-to-ear grin. Matt put his hand under my bent elbow and steered me toward the other dancers. Even through the fabric of my dress, his touch made my skin tingle with delight.

"You're a good dancer," he told me after a few minutes. "When you turned me down, I was afraid you didn't like to dance. At least, that's what I told myself so that I wouldn't take it personally."

Matt smiled sweetly and I knew I'd never be the same again if I couldn't have him for my own. So before I could think twice about what I was saying, I asked him, "Am I as good a dancer as Carol?"

"Better," he answered with an elflike grin. "If it matters."

I just smiled. Couldn't he tell that it mattered terribly?

As Matt led me around the dance floor (he was every bit as good a dancer as I'd dreamed), we didn't talk much, but every once in a while he'd lean his head back and look down at me with those gorgeous, smiling eyes of his.

That's when I'd get this special feeling, same as last Saturday night on our date, the feeling that Matt and I were the only two people in the world. I wished the song would never end.

But, of course it would, so I decided I'd better hurry up and point out that I hadn't been playing games when I'd turned him down earlier.

"Matt, I want to thank you for not being too stuck-up to ask me twice. Actually the explanation is kind of embarrassing, but I had a good reason for turning you down."

"You'd better," he teased.

I smiled back at him, then explained, "I do. See, I hurt my little toe during rehearsal this morning, and Dad made me promise no fast dancing tonight."

"But slow dancing is OK?"

"Right."

"Well, then, I hereby request the honor of dancing every single slow dance with you . . . as long as your little toe can take it, that is."

The way I felt upon hearing Matt's request, who needed feet? I was dancing on air.

"I . . . well . . . yes! I mean, it would be my honor, kind sir, to accept your request," I answered, imitating his courtly style.

And then, for one precious, endless moment, time stopped as Matt looked down at me as no boy had ever looked at me before. Just when I thought I might be about to get my first kiss, we both seemed to remember where we were—on a crowded dance floor, at a school function.

It seemed as though the music had stopped, and just as suddenly, started up again. But this time the rhythm to which we danced was set by the beat of our hearts, for now the only music that reached our ears was the music made by two people falling in love.

16

Although I never did get up the courage to ask him for the truth about last Saturday's date, all of my fears and doubts about Matt's affections scattered like stardust as he concentrated his attention entirely upon me. We spent the rest of the band's set together, right up until it was time for me to head backstage again.

"Just in case I turn into a pumpkin or something before I see you again, how about telling me yes to a date for tomorrow afternoon? I have some work to do on Uncle Charlie's plane in the morning, but then the rest of the day could be all ours," he told me.

"Could we go flying?" I asked hopefully. It was the first thing I thought of as I wanted so much to share Matt's favorite activity with him.

"I'm sorry, Maggie. Not tomorrow. Another time though, I promise. OK?"

Why was it that I kept getting the feeling Matt was putting me off on this issue? Either he wanted to take me flying with him or he didn't. My feelings a little hurt, I told him, "Sure, some other time," and excused myself to get ready for the next part of the fashion show.

"Dressed in this stunning navy-and-white, two-piece linen suit, Maggie Williams is ready for anything—from a dinner date to a birthday celebration . . ."

I made my entrance, semiconscious of the fact that Mrs. MacDonald had again tampered with the rehearsed commentary. She hadn't mentioned a birthday celebration that morning. When I saw the Blasters' singer, Tom, coming toward me from the opposite side of the stage, I knew I was in for it. He carried a microphone in his hand and wore a leering, Cheshire-cat grin all over his face.

". . .which could be considered something of a coincidence," continued Mrs. MacDonald, "as tonight just happens to be Maggie's 16th birthday!"

Believe me, I thought seriously about turning right around and walking out while the getting was good, because by then I had a pretty good idea of what was coming next. And sure enough, just as we met at center stage, Tom raised the microphone to his lips and began to sing:

"Happy birthday to you . . ."

He forcibly linked his arm through mine—I really had no choice in the matter without making a scene—and led me down the modeling ramp toward the audience while he continued singing the birthday song.

I was mad as a trapped hornet! If I didn't remain cordial toward Tom, I'd look like a fool. I still wanted to stomp right off the stage, but I hid my indignation in deference to Mrs. MacDonald and the fashion show. Why wreck her surprise just because Tom was a creep?

I'll have to give him this, he was a flawless performer. His timing was perfect all the way. He came to the final stanza just as we reached the end of the ramp. Just before the last line of the song, he paused, looked out at the audience, and gave them a wink, then leaned down real low so that his face was close to mine and said in a very suggestive voice: "See you after the show, Maggie."

Naturally, he was still speaking directly into the microphone so that everyone in the place could hear his words. It wasn't a question, but a statement, as though the arrangement were already settled. I wanted to hit him.

At last, he straightened back up and boomed out the last line: "Happy . . .birthday. . .to. . .you!"

I stared straight ahead at the faceless audience. For the benefit of the crowd, I tried my best to assume a natural-looking smile of appreciation.

Then all of a sudden, a pair of muscular arms enclosed me and before I knew what was happening, Tom had deposited a big, wet kiss smack in the center of my lips.

I wanted to die. No one else but Bren would have known but officially Tom's kiss qualified as my first! I never expected to get my first real kiss from someone I'd met only a couple of hours ago, and I certainly didn't expect it to happen in front of a few hundred people. The kids out front responded with applause and a lot of catcalls.

What stood out in my mind more than the actual kiss though was the sick realization that now, even if Matt ever did kiss me, he wouldn't be the first, as I'd hoped and dreamed. I prayed that Matt somehow had chosen just that moment to use the men's room or to step out for some air, so that at least he wouldn't know.

Then Tom whirled me around and we started back up the ramp. Just as I was thanking the heavens for small favors—at least our speedy exit would hide the fact that my face and neck had turned a brilliant scarlet—I saw his eyes light up and with a heart-sinking feeling, I knew that he wasn't finished with me after all.

He twirled me back around to face the audience and said, "Please forgive my inconsideration, everybody. I almost forgot to give the birthday girl a chance to speak for herself!"

As though he were addressing a helpless little six-year-old, he turned to me and said, "What charming little words of wit and wisdom would you like to share with us tonight, the night of your 16th birthday, Maggie?"

I wanted to murder him right there in front of everyone. If I didn't answer, I'd look like an idiot. If I did answer, I was sure to stutter and sound like an even bigger idiot.

I stood red-faced and mute for a few seconds that seemed like forever. This time, all of Mrs. Sutherlin's helpful tricks had vanished from my brain. Feeling slightly dizzy, I reached out with one hand, searching for something to steady myself. Instead I felt the bite of cold steel as Tom shoved the microphone into my hand.

I was stuck; I had to say something, so I sputtered out the first words that came to me: "I just want to thank everyone f-f-for c-c-coming tonight."

I knew it was bad, really bad, but at least I'd spoken aloud, so I shoved the microphone back toward Tom.

"All right! Isn't she just too much? To the point and on target!" Then with just the right touch of sincerity in his voice, he added, "From the band and me, too: Thanks for the great turnout tonight!"

By then, I figured the situation had dragged on long enough. I didn't care whether he followed or not, I was getting out of there. As I turned and headed for the exit, he gave his admiring audience one last wave and then caught up with me. At the top of the ramp, we peeled off in different directions, exiting at opposite sides of the stage. In spite of my embarrassment, it did register that the whole scene was right out of a Hollywood movie.

However, by then all I was thinking about was Matt, wondering what kind of reaction he'd had to the onstage spectacle.

Thinking back to the story he told me about how jealous he used to get over his old girl friend, I wondered if Tom's kiss had made him jealous. Deep down, I was thrilled by the idea of Matt liking me enough to be jealous. On the other hand, I realized Tom's behavior could definitely have worked against me.

Fearing that Matt could be out there somewhere thinking I was nothing but a shallow-minded flirt (ironically, the very perception I had of Carol), I decided to get out of my outfit right away and head directly for the dance floor in hopes I'd find Matt and have a chance to explain.

But before I could get that far, I got detoured by the other girls backstage. Most of them were flipping out with envy over the attention I'd received from Tom. Especially Carol.

"What was it like? Didn't you want to just melt into his arms?" she cooed wistfully.

"Not really," I replied.

They all treated me like some kind of celebrity, asking me lots of boring questions about Tom. How'd I meet him? Where were we going after the show? Didn't I feel lucky? And so on. I did my best to squelch their star-dust-coated illusions, but I have to admit that their excitement was contagious.

I made it back out front just as the band started up again. It was a fast song, so I walked around the edge of the crowded dance floor, looking for Matt.

I spotted the grown-ups first in a place I hadn't expected. They were out on the floor with the rest of the dancers, doing their best to imitate the movements of the youngsters around them. When the song ended, off the floor they came, laughing all the way to the refreshment table.

Avoiding them so I could continue looking for Matt, I finally spotted him on the far side of the dance floor. I was just getting close enough to call out his name when I saw a head of shining blond curls bouncing animatedly up and down beside Matt. Carol again.

Staying hidden behind a tall couple who'd two-stepped out in front of me, I maneuvered closer to Carol and Matt.

"I don't know how long they've known each other. Obviously, long enough," Carol was telling Matt. "Come on, Matt, forget about her. Let's dance."

I couldn't see Matt's face or hear if he answered her, but his body language was easy to read. Instead of looking down at Carol, he stood staring up at the band, right at Tom. Matt had his hands jammed deep in his pants pockets and held his shoulders in a rigid, unnatural postiton.

Matt *was* jealous of Tom, I realized suddenly. And Carol was simply feeding the fires of our misunderstanding.

"Matt . . . ," I called, determined to straighten things out immediately.

But before I could get out another word, Matt turned to me with an angry glare, then he grabbed Carol's arm roughly and the two of them disappeared into the crowd of dancers.

I debated briefly whether to follow them and force Matt to listen to the truth, but the more I thought about it, the angrier I became over Matt's willingness to listen to Carol and not to me.

But my anger only slightly abated the hurt I felt at seeing the two of them go off together. Certain that I'd lost Matt to Carol forever this time, like a vanquished soldier, I retreated.

As I sat at one of the dressing tables, wondering how Matt could have possibly taken Tom's obviously obtrusive come-on so seriously, I tried to force back the tears I felt brimming at the surface. With one more modeling set to do, all I needed was a smeared make-up job.

I went over and over the whole sorry scene, searching for clues to explain Matt's immature emotional display, when I realized it was Carol's words that provided the most logical explanation for Matt's behavior.

Clearly Carol had encouraged Matt to believe that Tom and I were already involved. It was understandable that Matt would feel shafted; after all, I'd apparently promised my attentions for the evening to two different boys. And Tom's embrace and kiss had certainly been a convincing performance.

So how was I going to convince Matt of the fallacies behind his assumptions? I doubted he'd even speak to me again.

As I stepped gingerly into the shorts outfit, my last outfit of the show (taking special care not to exert any pressure on my little toe), I wondered to myself how it could be that the night that had promised so much had turned so abruptly into the worst evening of my life.

17

I awoke the next morning with a start to the sound of the telephone ringing. I'd been dreaming of a romantic interlude with Matt. Even before I heard Dad answer the phone in the downstairs hallway, the events of the previous evening came back to me with heartsickening clarity.

After our last modeling set, once again I'd hurried out to the dance floor to find Matt. I was determined to make him listen to me, to make him understand the truth of the situation.

But I couldn't find him anywhere, so when I saw Sissie Hornell walking away from the refreshment table, I closed in on her, knowing that if anyone knew the where, when, or how (unfortunately I already knew the "why") of Matt's disappearance, she would be the one.

"The new boy? I think someone said he left just as your last modeling show got started."

Sissie thought he'd left alone. Thanks to our shared position, at least I knew he hadn't left with Carol. Carol's bikini, representing the freedom and fun of summer vacation, was the show-stopper finish to our program. At least I had the minor satisfaction of knowing that Matt hadn't been there to watch Carol show off her fantastic body.

"Telephone, Maggie," hollered Dad, yanking me back to the present.

It was Matt. I just knew it was. He'd called to apologize for his lack of faith in me; he'd reconfirm our afternoon date, telling me how he couldn't wait for us to be together again.

So much for dreaming—it wasn't Matt.

"Can you come in and work today, Maggie?" asked Mrs. MacDonald with a desperate sound to her voice. "I know it's short notice, but two of the Board girls who were scheduled to work today called in sick."

"What time would I need to be there?" I asked, looking down at the night clothes I still wore, noticing that it was already ten minutes after ten.

"We open at noon. Could you make it by 11:30 so I can go over a few of the basic cash-register procedures with you? I hate to throw on-the-job training at you like this, but Sundays are generally slow at our downtown store."

What could I do? I couldn't exactly turn Mrs. MacDonald down the first time she asked me to work unless I could provide her with a very convincing excuse of an important prior engagement. I doubted that my date with Matt could be considered a viable enough excuse especially since it was highly doubtful that the date still existed. So I told her I'd work.

While I showered, I debated on what to do about Matt. Recalling the plans Matt had outlined for today, I knew he'd be leaving for Lake Hood soon. Was I brave enough to try reaching him at home before he left? My knees started quaking at the idea.

Telling myself I had a perfectly justifiable excuse for calling him, my fingers quivered as I dialed the Brennans' number, which I'd gotten from new listings. However, all my nervousness was for nothing. Mrs. Brennan informed me that Matt had left early, more than two hours before. When she asked who was calling and if there were a message, I gave her my name and asked her to tell Matt that I had to work today. That way I knew he'd know where he could find me. If he wanted to, that is.

I arrived at Farland's to find that Mrs. MacDonald had been called away by an emergency at the other store. She'd left Ms. Grimley in charge of initiating my salesclerk instruction. It was my observation that the lady had no sympathy for beginners, at least not for this one. She rattled off the procedures and departmental codes that I was expected to memorize faster than a computer print-out.

And contrary to Mrs. MacDonald's earlier assurances, I think the whole world chose that afternoon to shop at Farland's downtown store.

I kept searching the faceless crowd of customers for the one person who could have turned my whole day around. But he never showed up.

At school the next day, I saw Matt in the halls twice; both times he spotted me first and managed to avoid me.

On our way home, Bren tried to cheer me up with talk about the girl-boy party we planned to throw at her house in two weeks. I didn't even care if we had the party any more, since Matt obviously wouldn't be my date.

As if I weren't miserable enough, Cherub's health had showed no visible improvement on Sunday. So on Monday, while I was at school, Dad and Cherub made another trip to Dr. Hill's . . . I never even got to tell Cherub good-bye.

When I walked into the front entry of our town house and Cookie was the only one to meet me, Dad didn't have to say the words: the hurt in his red eyes told me that Cherub wouldn't be coming home this time.

Now that some time has passed, I can accept the fact that Dad and Dr. Hill made the right decision for Cherub. But at that moment, all I could think of was that earlier in the day, Cherub had been alive and now he was dead.

For the rest of the week, I became morbidly obsessed with Cherub's death. I couldn't stop tormenting myself with heartbreaking visions of little Cherub looking up at Dr. Hill with a pathetic, trying-to-understand-look in his big, brown eyes; trusting Dr. Hill, even as he received the deadly shot. And then I'd watch him lie down and go to sleep, never to wake again.

These kinds of dire imaginings would in turn bring on crying bouts that ended only when the escape of sleep finally overcame me.

Dad easily consented to my skipping school the next day. The only remedy that helped at all was to keep myself mesmerized in front of the daytime soaps. I went to bed early, seeking the solace of unconsciousness.

Morning brought the good news that Matt had called me the previous evening, but Dad hadn't wanted to wake me. Thinking I could tough it out—especially because I figured that since Matt had called, he must be ready to talk things out—I told Dad I'd give school a try that day.

But at school, I found out that my emotions were still highly unstable. Even the most indirect references to an animal or illness triggered an uncontrollable flood of tears, whether right in the middle of a class or at lunch, it didn't seem to matter. I was embarrassed by the silly and child-ish-sounding explanation whispered behind my back: "Her dog died." It seemed no one truly understood the grief I felt.

After third period, I asked Bren if she would mind driving me home at lunch; my eyes were swollen and red and my nose too stuffy to breathe properly. She agreed without hesitation and said if there were anything she could do, or if I just wanted to talk about it, she would be there.

The funny thing was that I didn't feel like talking to anyone any more, not even Bren. So when I went to collect my coat and a few books from my locker and rounded the corner to see Matt standing there waiting for me, this time it wasn't because I felt too tongue-tied to talk. I'd simply lost the desire.

"I was wrong," he said to me when I got closer. Without saying a word, I reached around him and dialed my locker combination.

"I'm sorry, Maggie . . . forgive me?"

Again the tears started swelling. My emotions on the brink of disinte-gration, it was all I could to to speak coherently.

"I'd never seen Tom before in my life and none of it was my idea . . . not the singing, the kiss, or meeting him after the show," I defended. "As a matter of fact," I told him, building up steam, "it was the worst birthday of my life."

"I know, I know," he said apologetically. "Bren explained everything." Matt took my books and walked with me toward the exit to the student parking lot where Bren would be waiting. "You didn't answer my question, Maggie," he persisted. "Will you forgive me?"

"Of course." Overjoyed about our reconciliation but still desperately sad about Cherub, I wanted to explain why I was about to burst into tears any second. "Matt . . . Cherub . . . ," but I couldn't go on.

Matt dropped my books and opened his arms. I fell against him, sobbing uncontrollably, still trying to form words to explain about Cherub.

"Sssh," he told me. "Bren also told me about Cherub."

After my crying had at last spent itself, he pulled a handkerchief out of his back pocket and handed it to me. As I blew and sniffed and wiped my dripping nose, he said, "Listen, I know Bren's waiting to take you home. You go on now and I'll call you tonight. Then we can talk, OK?"

I nodded my head, he gave me one more quick embrace, and then walked me out to where Bren waited.

On the way home, I told Bren I really didn't want to go through with our plans for a party. She agreed quietly. Then I remembered to thank her for setting Matt straight.

"You're not mad at me for interfering?"

"Not this time," I said, managing a smile of gratitude for my friend.

18

Dad had wanted me to stay home the rest of the week. And I'd have taken him up on his offer, but now that Matt wasn't mad at me any more, and since the following week was spring vacation, I returned to school on Friday to collect the homework I'd missed and the assignments made for over the break. (I'll never understand why teachers always give us homework when it's supposed to be a vacation.) But before the day even got started, I began to wish I'd listened to Dad.

When I rounded the corner headed for my locker, whom should I see but Matt and Bren, huddled close together at Bren's and my locker, examining a piece of paper that Bren held in her hands. It wasn't just their being together that upset me; after all, Bren was the one who'd patched things up between Matt and me. What unnerved me was the intentness with which they regarded whatever was on the paper they were sharing.

"Now there's a conspiracy if I ever saw one," I said as I approached them. They both jumped a mile when they saw who it was.

"Hi, Maggie," said Matt. "Bren and I were just talking about you, wondering if you'd make it back today. We were just going over some . . .math problems."

He looked at Bren as if for confirmation, then back at me. When neither of us answered, he darted a glance at his watch and then, as if he were late, he said, "Oops, I've got to get going, see you two later."

And off he ran like a fleeing criminal. Bren shoved the piece of paper she and Matt had been studying into her notebook before I could see what was written on it.

"What's going on, Bren?" I asked her suspiciously.

"What do you mean?" she replied as she finished collecting her books for first period. "You know I have trouble with math. Matt's a real whiz with numbers."

In spite of her calm and reasonable explanation, it seemed to me that Bren was making a special effort to act nonchalant about Matt's presence. I guess my suspicions were rather apparent.

"Now wait a minute, Maggie. You don't think there might be something going on between Matt and me, do you?"

"Well, if I remember correctly, you were the one so flipped-out over the new boy the first time you saw him."

"Maggie! Even if you didn't know I already like Randy, I can't believe you could stand here and accuse me of trying to steal Matt. Tell you what, I'll just chalk it up to your unbalanced emotional state and we'll forget all about it."

"Show me the piece of paper you were looking at, then we'll forget it," I said stubbornly.

"What? You mean you don't even trust your best friend? Well, then you just forget it!" And off she stomped without letting me look at the paper.

I thought about the incident all morning. For as much as I paid attention to my teachers, I might as well have stayed home. I finally decided I'd been wrong to accuse Bren, but that no matter how much I liked him, I really didn't know Matt well enough to judge his guilt or innocence. Why had he run off so fast? He hadn't even asked to have lunch with me or anything.

Thinking that Matt's and my relationship suffered from a definite lack of communication, I decided to meet him at his last class before lunch to make sure we had a chance to talk.

My P.E. class actually got out early for a change, so I was waiting at the door to Matt's class when the bell rang. I'd completely forgotten that his fourth period was one of the classes he shared with Carol.

Matt and Carol came out the door together behind a big crowd of kids so that at first they didn't spot me. They were laughing at something Carol had said. She was leaning against Matt as they walked, waving her hand in the air and then touching his arm, presumably to emphasize her point.

The first thought that flashed through my mind was how comfortable they looked together and what a good-looking couple they made.

My next thought was how I'd like to show them both. It was obvious that Carol had taken advantage of my brief absence to work on Matt's affections; however, it didn't look like Matt was trying very hard to fend her off.

When I couldn't stand watching them any longer, I turned to run away. Apparently Matt spotted me at the very same moment because I heard him call out my name. But by then I felt the tears begin to spill over, so I kept on going, speeding up my pace as I weaved in and out of the mass of kids headed for lunch.

I spent the lunch hour in the girls' lavatory. The rest of the afternoon, I played hide-and-seek with Matt. I was determined to avoid him. When I saw him waiting at my locker after lunch, I went to Mr. Glasier's class without the appropriate books rather than give Matt his chance to try convincing me that he and Carol were nothing but friends. I liked Matt more than I'd ever liked anyone in my life, but I wouldn't be made a fool. Especially by the likes of Carol Conners.

He even tried to get to me through my best friend. "Maggie, be reasonable," she told me on our way home. "They were only walking out of class together; you aren't going with him, you know."

"I know, and that's one thing I can be thankful for. You know what else? Remember all the stories I told you about his old girl friend always trying to make him jealous? I think it was a two-way street; she was probably just trying to even the score."

"Oh, Maggie, he likes you. I know he does."

"Why? Because he told you so? Can't you see he's not exactly the trust-worthy sort? Look, Bren, I know I was unreasonably jealous this morning at our locker and I apologize. But finding him with Carol is a different story."

We continued to argue all the way to my house. As I climbed out of Betsy, I told Bren, "From now on, don't bring Matt up, don't even mention his name to me, OK?" She gave me a look of exasperation, an exaggerated sigh, and then sped off.

When I walked in the door, Dad informed me that he had invited Mrs. Sutherlin out for dinner at the Crow's Nest, one of Anchorage's ritziest restaurants, dark and intimate with a breathtaking view of Cook Inlet.

Actually I was relieved that I'd have the house to myself for the evening, I needed to be alone to work through the bitterness I felt over Matt's false pretenses. I even turned down Bren and Randy's invitation to accompany them to the movies. The last thing I felt like was being a third wheel to Bren and Randy's twosome.

So Cookie and I spent the evening in front of the tube, most of the time from the kitchen as I consoled myself with chocolate-chip cookies, popcorn, and the last half of a pint of ice cream.

The phone rang four different times, each time for a lengthy period, but I refused to answer it in case it was Matt. I didn't know whether it was overly presumptuous to assume he'd try to reach me, but at least I got a small degree of satisfaction pretending he was calling. *Let him think I'm out on a date with someone else*, I told myself consolingly. I couldn't bear to think of the probable truth—that he and Carol were out together somewhere, having fun, kissing.

I fell asleep on the couch sometime during the late movie. When Dad got home, he helped me up the stairs to my room, chattering all the way about what a wonderful evening he and Mrs. Sutherlin had had. (I noticed he was calling her Ann.) I was still sleeping soundly when Dad woke me the next morning, saying I had a phone call. I hadn't even heard the phone ring.

Memory of the previous evening floated up from my subconscious.

Still assuming it was Matt, I told him I didn't want to talk to anyone. But Dad said, "It's Bren. She says it's important."

"I know this is short notice and you don't have to say yes, but would you consider working for me this afternoon and tomorrow too? Randy wants to take me camping."

It took me only a minute to remember that I faced a very lonely and boring weekend so I told her yes.

"Oh, Maggie, thanks so much. I'll call Mrs. MacDonald and get her approval; I'm sure she won't mind. How was your evening?" she asked tentatively.

"Quiet. But Dad had a date with Mrs. Sutherlin. You should have seen him! He was in the bathroom getting ready for more than an hour. I think he really wanted to impress her."

"Of course, and he probably succeeded," she answered. Then her voice got deeper, the way it does when she's speaking of a serious matter. "How would you feel if they got married, Maggie? If Mrs. Sutherlin were to become your stepmother?"

"Bren! It was only a date—their *first* date!"

But inwardly, I believe that even then I already had accepted the idea. For one thing, I'm not in the habit of playing matchmaker, yet I'd eagerly gone ahead with Bren's scheme.

Secondly, although no one could ever replace my mother, I realized that a woman's influence around our house and, most especially, a loving companion for Dad, would not be a bad thing.

Driving me to work later that morning, Dad's enthusiastic reporting of his evening confirmed my thoughts on the subject.

"Actually, Ann and I have a number of interests in common," he elaborated. "We talked until the restaurant was ready to close. Which reminds me, one of our topics of conversation centered on your friend Matt and his family."

I almost choked on the gum I was chewing when I heard Matt's name. Talk about being haunted by someone!

"Ann and I agree that it would be a nice gesture to offer the Brennans some good old-fashioned Alaskan hospitality," he went on. I gripped the edge of my seat, knuckles white, the pit of my stomach twisting and churning in anticipation of Dad's next words.

"Ann offered to come over and help with the meal preparation so that we could invite Matt and his whole family over to our place for dinner. We were thinking about next Friday. . . ."

"No! I mean. . .I can't do it that night." Panic-stricken, I tossed out the first excuse that came to my mind. "I think I have to work next weekend," I told him.

"Oh," he said, disappointed. I felt bad shooting down Dad's first real effort to become more socially outgoing. But I couldn't stand the thought of a forced confrontation with Matt. Even without a confrontation, assuming the presence of the others would prevent that, it would be too difficult to watch all evening what I could never have. What I didn't want, I reminded myself sternly.

"OK, Ms. Busy, how about if you check your schedule and let us know what evening might be convenient?"

I agreed, figuring at least I was off the hook for a little while, until I had time to figure out a more permanent excuse.

I arrived at work only to find that the day held yet another unwanted surprise. It turned out to be Carol's first day at Farland's and since naturally we were assigned to the same department, guess who got appointed to break her in on the cash register. Amazingly enough, I found Carol decently civil to me. For once, *she* was the fish out of water.

"I don't think I'll ever get the hang of this code business, Maggie. This isn't a cash register, it's a computer!"

"Don't worry, Carol," I assured her, "by tonight you'll have this machine humming and buzzing."

And while I'm teaching you how to run the machine, maybe I can pick up some pointers on how to manage boys, I thought to myself as I watched Carol assisting a cute boy who'd come wandering into the department with an utterly lost look on his face. Sure enough, 15 minutes later, he left not only with an armload of purchases, but with Carol's phone number and a tentative date.

"Carol, I don't know how you do it. I mean, of course you're beautiful and everything, but how do you manage to act so natural around boys?"

She just looked at me and shrugged indifferently, as if to say, either you've got it or you don't.

But at the end of the day, she offered me a ride home and as we headed for her car, Carol said, "You know, Maggie, you can't be doing everything so wrong if Matt Brennan is after you."

Her statement caught me completely off-guard. All day long, there had been an unspoken agreement between us to avoid the subject of one Matt Brennan. And I certainly didn't believe that Matt was "after" me; in fact, the situation was just the opposite.

"What do you mean?" I asked her. What did she know about Matt's feelings that I didn't?

"Do I have to spell it out for you?" she answered, unlocking the passenger door for me. "He wants to impress you in the worst way."

I didn't believe her; she had some kind of trick up her sleeve, I was sure of it. "How do you know? Did he tell you that?"

Once inside the car, Carol wouldn't look at me. With a cement-stiff expression on her face, she stared out the front window, acting as though she were about to lose her self-control. The tension in the air was so intense I had an impulse to jump out of the car and run. At the same time, anticipation over her next words had me glued to the seat.

"Not in so many words; he didn't have to." No longer attempting to restrain her bitterness, Carol turned her head, let her blazing eyes burn deep into mine and said, "The girl a boy likes is always the last to know."

19

Needless to say, the drive home was an uncomfortable one. I took advantage of the long periods of silence by reviewing in detail the entire history of Matt's and my short relationship.

What I decided was that we had both been guilty of critical misjudgments at crucial times. I only hoped that this last misunderstanding hadn't caused irreparable damage.

Suddenly I realized that an idea that had earlier seemed insufferable could actually provide the perfect arena for our reconciliation. Just as soon as Carol dropped me off, I got started on renewing Dad's dinner party idea.

"I'm home, Dad. And guess what? I don't have to work next Friday night, after all. I was thinking about the old days in Oregon, when you and Mom used to invite family friends over for dinner on a regular basis . . .well. . .I think inviting the Brennans is a superb idea."

"Why, thank you, daughter. I'm pleased to learn that you approve, after all. Judging by your initial reaction, I'd begun to think I'd done something wrong again."

"Oh, Dad," I whined.

I was dying to call Bren to tell her about the dinner and to apologize once again for my stubbornness (and Bren was the one who was supposed to be the stubborn one in our friendship!). But of course, she was still camping with Randy and wouldn't be home until Sunday night.

Remembering the phone calls I hadn't answered Friday night, I wondered if, in fact, it had been Matt trying to call, and if so, why he wasn't still trying to get hold of me, I almost dialed his number a hundred times but I didn't want to chase him and, because I wanted one last assurance that he liked me as much as I liked him, somehow I managed to resist the temptation to punch out those seven magic little numbers.

I stayed extremely busy at work the next day, which helped the time to pass. When Mrs. MacDonald asked if I could work the following Saturday night, I was so relieved that she hadn't requested the night of our dinner party that I said yes without a second thought.

When I got home and found out that Dad hadn't even extended the invitation yet, I threw a fit. He must have thought my reaction was a little overboard. How was he to know that I was hoping his call might initiate an earlier reconciliation between Matt and me.

When at last he made the call, I could tell very little from Dad's end of the conversation. Finally I heard him saying, "I'll be sure to tell her."

"Tell me what?" I said the minute he'd hung up. But he wanted to make me sweat it a little.

"I said *her*, not *Maggie*. How do you know I wasn't referring to another female? To Ann, for instance?" His smile was full of mischief as he sauntered off toward the kitchen.

I followed him, thinking to myself that he sure had Ann on his mind a lot lately. Not that I minded; he seemed more his old, cheerful self these days.

"Dad," I whined, "what did she say?"

"She asked me to apologize for her."

"Apologize for what?"

"Apparently Matt left early Saturday on a fly-out fishing trip for a few days. He'd asked her to tell you where he was, if you called."

Which I hadn't, I thought to myself. So that *had* been Matt calling Friday night, probably to tell me about his plans, which naturally he hadn't had a chance to tell me about on Friday, because I'd so adeptly avoided him all day long.

"But the fishermen are experiencing some pretty nasty weather out there in the bush and she was supposed to relay a radio-phone message she got from him this morning. Matt's uncle and the flight instructor don't think the weather will lift for at least a few days. He wanted her to let you know."

Then Dad poured himself a fresh cup of coffee and strolled off toward his office, leaving me alone with my conflicting emotions.

Although I was disappointed to learn that Matt would be gone most of the vacation, I was at once relieved and elated to know that he'd been thinking of me enough to make sure I wasn't worried about him. But what genuinely puzzled me was the information that a flight instructor had accompanied Matt and his uncle. What did that mean?

Before I could reach any conclusions, the phone rang and it was Bren, home from her camping trip.

"When did he say he'd be back?" she asked, after I'd filled her in on Matt's trip and what Carol had told me.

"There's no way to know when to expect him; it depends on the weather. Hopefully no later than Friday as that's the night we've invited the Brennans over for dinner."

"You've got to be kidding, Maggie. Do you know how many kids are in the Brennan family?"

"No, but Mrs. Sutherlin will be helping me."

"Mrs. Sutherlin? Guess your dad's date must have gone pretty well."

"Guess so."

"Well, I'm glad you'll have help because Matt told me he has three brothers and one set of twin sisters."

It bothered me a little that Bren knew more about Matt's family than I. I couldn't help flashing back to last Friday when I'd surprised them at Bren's and my locker. Why did it still seem as if Matt were more willing to open up to Carol or Bren than to me?

The week dragged by uneventful as ever. Each day, I told myself that this would be the day that Matt returned, but the weather front that covered southwest Alaska didn't budge. At last, on Thursday night, I got a call from Mrs. Brennan, who said she'd received word from the camp that the skies seemed to be clearing and the three fishermen planned to return the next morning. Not a day too soon, I thought thankfully.

Right at the agreed-upon time on Friday morning, Ann (she'd asked me to use her first name outside of school) came up our walkway loaded down with an overflowing sack of groceries in each arm. I rushed to greet her at the front door so she wouldn't have to ring the bell with her nose.

"Thank you," she said breathlessly, as I took one of the bags from her. "I probably overdid it on the groceries. But I'm used to cooking for one, so I wanted to make sure I had enough for all of us."

"I've got coffee ready. Would you like some?" I asked her as we headed for the kitchen.

"Yes, I'd love…"

But before Ann could finish her sentence, in walked Dad with a cup of steaming coffee in his hand.

"For Madame," he said, with a courtly bow and his winning smile.

Ann's bright laughter filled the house as she accepted his offering. "Just what I've been looking for," she teased. "A man who anticipates my every desire."

As discreetly as possible, I disappeared into the living room to roust Cookie from her position of comfort underneath the coffee table. I thought that Dad and Ann would appreciate a few minutes alone.

Cookie had undergone extraordinary changes in the two weeks since Cherub had left us. At first, she'd done nothing much but mope around the house, mourning for Cherub. However, nourished by a double dose of affection from Dad and me, my submissive underdog was gradually transforming into a possessive watchdog.

Dr. Hill assured Dad and me that the changes in Cookie's personality were a natural occurrence. Without Cherub around, Cookie took over the role of family protector.

Cookie was winning our wrestling match when Dad and Ann walked in to see what all the commotion was about.

"Help!" I sputtered, trying to dodge Cookie's attempts to give me a big, fat, slobbery kiss. "OK, Cookie, let me up."

As I scrambled up from the floor, Ann asked, "Ready to begin our soon-to-be-famous spaghetti sauce?"

"Ready!"

Dad winked at me and said, "Well, then, I believe I'll slip off to the office and let you girls attend to your duties."

"Duties!" protested Ann and I in unison.

Dad assured us he was only joking but disappeared just the same.

Ann and I spent the next three hours preparing authentic Italian meat-ball sauce. No wonder I always used the mix packets. But it was fun working with Ann in the kitchen and periodically Dad would pop in to check up on our progress, sample the product, and give us his valued opinion. It crossed my mind that the three of us had already begun to feel like a real family.

It took me all afternoon to figure out that I didn't have a thing to wear that evening. Now that I was finally going to see Matt again—the past week had seemed like forever—I was so nervous I could hardly think straight.

Nothing in my closet satisfied me, so I crossed my fingers as I dialed Bren's number, hoping she'd be home and that she'd have some suggestions.

"What about your maroon Esprit sweater? The vee neckline in the back is really attractive. It looks good with those matching jeans."

"I thought of that outfit but the sweater is dirty and besides, I was thinking of something a little more feminine, something that Dad and Ann would approve of."

"A full skirt and soft sweater?" suggested Bren.

"Perfect. Only none of my skirts and sweaters go together any more. I dumped grape juice on my white silk and angora sweater. And that's the only top I had to wear with my blue jersey skirt."

"You mean the superfull one with the big pockets? I'll bet my new sweater is the same shade of blue. Want to try it?"

Bren and I can't trade skirts, dresses, or pants because of an obvious height discrepancy, but our tops usually work for each other. Bren wears one size larger so her things look soft and drapey on me, just the way I like them.

"Oh, Bren, you sure you wouldn't mind? You just got it last week."

"I wouldn't have offered if I did, silly. Shall I zoom over right now so you can try it? I've got to get ready for my date with Randy pretty soon."

"Still Randy, huh?"

"Looks like he's beaten the ol' love-'em-and-leave-'em queen herself, doesn't it? Would you believe I still get butterflies in my stomach before he comes to pick me up? Say, have you heard from Matt yet?"

"No, but I got another message from his mother. They should be back today sometime." Then I remembered the puzzling part of Mrs. Brennan's first message. "He flew out with his uncle and a flight instructor," I told her.

"What? I thought Matt already knew how to fly."

"So did I," I answered. "But I've been thinking about it, I don't remember Matt's ever once actually coming right out and saying he had a pilot's license. And every time I've asked him to take me flying, he's always had an excuse."

Actually I'd been thinking about it a lot. If my suspicions proved true, then Matt had been deliberately deceitful.

"Well, I'm sure he'll be able to explain everything when you see him tonight."

"I was hoping he'd call before then." It was the least he could do after making me wait all week.

"I wouldn't get your hopes up too high, Maggie. You know how practical boys are. He probably figures there's no need to call since he'll be seeing you tonight. But I bet he tries to make it up to you," she said, sounding mysteriously certain. "I bet he asks you to go out with him tomorrow night."

"I hope not because I already promised Mrs. MacDonald I'd work."

"What? You're kidding!"

"No, I promised last weekend when I filled in for you," I answered, wondering why it should bother Bren that I'd be working again this weekend. "Apparently Mrs. MacDonald had received quite a few requests to have Saturday night off. She asked if I'd mind filling in."

"Mrs. MacDonald! I should've. . ."

"Should've what?" I asked, puzzled over Bren's strange response.

"Oh, never mind," she answered, obviously preoccupied with other thoughts. "Listen, I've got to make a couple of calls, then I'll be right over with the sweater, OK?"

"See you."

I pushed Bren's unusual behavior to the back of my mind so I could concentrate on the rest of my preparations for the upcoming evening. I felt certain that Bren's sweater was just what my skirt needed.

The only worry looming heavily on my mind was whether or not Matt would find the girl inside those clothes suitably attractive.

20

Amazingly enough, by 5:30, Ann and I were heading for the living room to take a break before our guests arrived at six o'clock. Dinner preparations were as far along as they could get, and the table was set with Mom's good china that I'd unpacked earlier in the week; this would be the first time we'd used it since our move.

Ann and I had set the dining room table for six: Mr. and Mrs. Brennan, Dad, Ann, Matt, and myself. The five children, all grade-school age and under, would sit in the kitchen at the snack bar. Naturally they got to eat from Dad's and my everyday dinnerware.

A couple of hours earlier, Dad had stepped out from his study and left the house, returning with a beautiful spring bouquet. Flowers are a luxury item up here, and this bouquet was resplendent with orchids, roses, baby's breath, lilies, and daisies. Ann and I were both moved by Dad's thoughtfulness.

"Oh, Bill, they're the perfect finishing touch!"

I put a hand to my neck to caress Mother's pearls—I wore them for good luck—and smiled to myself at Dad's consideration. Just a week or two ago, he would have never thought of the flowers. It was Ann's positive influence again. I wondered if she knew.

At only a few minutes past six o'clock, the doorbell rang and Cookie let out several supposedly ferocious barks. This was another one of her new tricks since Cherub had left us; she'd begun to announce the arrival of strangers with her cute little arf-arfs.

I was afraid Dad would ask me to answer the door, but instead he rose from his chair to greet our guests himself. Mr. and Mrs. Brennan came through the door first, with two preschoolers who were obviously the identical twins. Three grade-school-age boys of ascending height followed.

"Welcome," said Dad. "Come on in."

As Ann rose from the couch and walked over for introductions, Dad and Mr. and Mrs. Brennan—Jim and Gayle— shook hands. The Brennan children were introduced as Mike, Mitch, Melvin, Julie, and Christie. Meanwhile, I sat quietly, contemplating a nervous breakdown: Matt was nowhere in sight.

"And this is my daughter, Maggie," said Dad, with a broad sweep of his arm as he tried to include me in the little gathering.

"It's so good to meet you, dear," said Mrs. Brennan. "We've been hearing your name frequently around our household the last couple of weeks."

"Matt sends along his apologies for not arriving with the rest of us," said Mr. Brennan. He was a tall man and I could see where Matt had gotten his exceptional-looking blue eyes.

But Mr. Brennan's resemblance to Matt was no substitute for the real thing. Why hadn't Matt shown up? If Mrs. Brennan had heard Matt talking about me, didn't that mean he liked me?

"Don't worry, honey," Mrs. Brennan told me. "Matt should be along shortly. He and his uncle just got into town this morning, and Matt's had an extremely busy day—I'm sure he'll want to tell you all about it himself."

"He got home just as we were leaving," added Mr. Brennan. "Naturally, he had to get spiffed up before coming to see Maggie," he said, giving the other adults a knowing grin.

I felt myself blushing. I certainly hoped the grown-ups wouldn't persist in teasing us all evening. I had second thoughts about the seating arrangement—maybe eating in the kitchen with Matt's brothers and sisters would have been more comfortable.

Ann turned out to be a natural hostess. She served the adults coffee, and then corralled the kids into the kitchen where Cookie kept them entertained. Sitting with the adults, listening to their conversation, I was the only one who felt left out.

Thirty minutes later, just as the adults were discussing how much longer to wait for Matt, the doorbell rang. "I'll get it," I announced, leaping from the couch. No one even tried to beat me to the door.

Bursting with anticipation, I took a deep breath and then yanked the front door wide open. Before me stood the handsomest boy I'd ever laid eyes on.

"For you, Mademoiselle," said Matt, holding out before him a dozen long-stemmed red roses.

"For me?"

I simply stood there dumbfounded. No boy had ever given me flowers before. When he thrust them into my hands, my impulse was to reach out and give him the biggest hug of his life, but then I remembered we had an audience behind us. Besides I also remembered hearing that the boy's supposed to make the first move. If it hadn't been for the adults' presence, I'm afraid I'd have been tempted to break the rules.

"Sorry I'm late," Matt whispered as I motioned him inside. "I can explain everything."

"That's OK," I told him, "just as long as you'll forgive me for acting so childishly last Friday."

Still standing in the entryway, he looked at me tenderly and said, "I ought to have been more considerate of your feelings. We'll talk about it all later.'"

I took Matt's coat and then we joined the others. Dinner went off without a hitch. Everybody raved about the spaghetti; kids and adults alike loved the chocolate cake I'd baked for dessert.

The only truly uncomfortable moment came when at last Matt was forced to reveal the truth about his status as a pilot.

"How was you fishing trip, Matt," asked Dad, midway through dessert. Dad himself is not much of a sportsman so I knew the question was a polite attempt to bring Matt and me into the conversation, which had been centered predominantly around the interests of the adults.

"Great, Mr. Williams. Uncle Charlie and I caught and released at least a few dozen rainbows over five pounds."

"Maggie tells me that you're quite the pilot, Matt," offered Ann.

"Well, I certainly do love to fly," said Matt, giving me a peculiar side-glance.

I watched him intently, full of dread that my suspicion that he'd deceived me would prove true. Then Mr. Brennan, innocently proud of his son's accomplishment, let the cat out of the bag.

"Oh, come on, Matt, quit with all the humble malarkey. Aren't you going to tell these folks the good news? If you don't, I will."

Matt looked at me apologetically, then said to everybody, "I passed my check ride today."

"What he means," interpreted Mr. Brennan, "is that as of 4 P.M. today, Matt became a full-fledged licensed pilot!"

Matt knew I was watching him, but he wouldn't look back at me. Once again, I was reminded of how little we really knew each other.

"Matt's so modest," observed his mother, misinterpreting the pain and embarrassment all over his face. "Actually, he's been flying for years, but until we moved up here where he's had access to his uncle's plane, lessons on a regular basis weren't possible."

"Congratulations, Matt," said Dad. "Now that I know a real pilot, I'll have to see about getting you to fly me over some of the volcanic formations on the Alaskan Peninsula."

Just like Dad, always thinking of his research. Naturally the conversation drifted on to Dad's latest project. As the adults pursued a discussion of the benefits accrued from the scientific investigation of predicting seismic disturbances, Matt leaned over and whispered, "I can explain, Maggie, I promise."

"OK," I answered warily, thinking to myself that there was more than just the pilot issue that would require an explanation. For starters, why Matt always seemed to prefer hanging around Bren or Carol and was willing to talk about himself to them, but not to me.

So although I felt very grown-up sitting at the candlelit dining table with the adults, I was dying to have the chance to talk to Matt alone. But the after-dinner chatter seemed to drag on. Learning that Matt had allowed me and everyone else at school to believe he'd had his license when he didn't disturbed me so much that I couldn't even finish my dessert. And it was chocolate!

There was still a dusky light outside when we all finally stood to push our chairs back from the table. Matt suggested that he and I take Cookie and Jam, who had been stowed in the back of Matt's pickup during dinner, for a walk. Right away, Matt's brothers and sisters piped up with, "We want to go, too," but Mrs. Brennan interceded for us, telling them, "No, you stay here where I can keep an eye on you."

Matt and I leashed up the dogs and headed down the sidewalk. I was so full of questions that I walked beside him in silence, unsure of where to begin.

But I didn't have to worry about conversation openers; Matt started apologizing the minute we got out the door.

"Maggie, I wanted to tell you before the others; I was supposed to get back to town early in the week so I'd have plenty of time to take my check ride and tell you about it first. But we got weathered in and then my instructor got me a last-minute appointment this afternoon and, well. . .I'd made a promise to myself to get the license out of the way before spring break was over."

"But, Matt, why did you let everybody believe you already had your license?"

"I never once told you or anyone I had a legal license," he said defensively. "Everybody just seemed to want to believe it."

He paused, then added somewhat devilishly, "Besides, it'll serve Carol right when she finds out, don't you think? I told you I know her kind. She's the one who spread that rumor and the only reason she's been after me was so I'd take her flying and then she could brag to all her friends."

"That still doesn't make it right."

"I know. OK, there's more." He took a deep breath and we stopped on the sidewalk for a minute. "I was hoping *you'd* be impressed too. I like you, Maggie. I like you a lot. I think I've liked you since my first day at Ridgeway when we ran into each other. Almost everything I've done since then has been centered around impressing you."

"Including hanging around Carol?"

He took another deep breath, reached for my hand, and held it between his. The scent of his musky, masculine cologne teased my senses, weakening my resolve to be tough with him.

"Carol's been a reliable crutch for a somewhat shy new kid," he admitted. "She was easy for me to be around right from the start, even if she's not a nice person a lot of the time. As I told you, she reminds me of my old girlfriend. It sounds stupid but it was a lot easier for me to talk to Carol or to your friend Bren than to you, because I didn't care what they thought about me—only what you thought."

I didn't know what to say. Matt's testimonial had almost brought me to tears. Then he asked me a question for which I had no trouble finding the answer.

"Maggie, now that I'm truly legal, I can finally ask you to go flying with me. I'd like you to be the first. Is it a deal?"

"A deal," I beamed, extending my hand to shake on it. But instead of shaking my hand when he took hold of it, Matt pulled me up next to him, encircling me with a tender embrace.

With my head pressed against his chest, I could hear the beating of Matt's heart as I stared cross-eyed into his blue tweed sweater. Then Matt placed one hand gently under my chin and lifted my face toward his. Gazing lovingly into my eyes, he whispered, "Maggie..." and then his lips met mine like a gentle promise.

And so, I got my first real kiss from Matt, after all. Because, next to Matt's kiss, Tom's didn't exist.

We resumed our walk, making our last turn around the block a slow one. We were almost home when Cookie started tugging on her leash; it was a routine thing with us that I let her loose to run the final stretch home.

I was reaching down to unhook Cookie's leash when Matt fulfilled the rest of Bren's prediction:

"I've got an idea. Let's go see a movie tomorrow night, OK, Maggie?"

I started to say yes but suddenly remembered my commitment to Mrs. MacDonald and so, although it broke my heart, I had to tell him no.

"What? You're working on a Saturday night? Don't those shops ever close down?"

"Hardly. All the dateless girls in town have to have *something* to do," I teased, thinking how lucky I was to be moving out of their ranks.

"But Maggie, can't you get someone to work for you?"

I loved the sound of desperation in his voice; I still couldn't believe he really liked me that much. But that didn't solve my dilemma.

"Apparently there's something going on tomorrow night because a lot of Board members requested the night off."

"So there's no one to fill in for you," he said, with obvious frustration.

Actually I thought his disappointment seemed rather out of proportion, especially since I'd told him I had Sunday night free. After waiting this long, postponing our date by one day didn't seem *that* disastrous to me. But for some reason, Matt was determined to see me the next night.

He was still grumbling about it when we said good-night. He asked me once more if there weren't some way I could get out of working the evening shift. When I had to reply in the negative, I began to have second thoughts about the supposed glamour of my new position.

Now that I finally had Matt, I didn't want anything to come between us.

21

At first, I thought I was still dreaming when, half-asleep, I picked up the receiver and heard Matt's voice on the other end of the line.

"Hi, Maggie. Let me drive you to work this afternoon, I've got a surprise for you...hey, you awake?"

"Getting there," I mumbled. "What time is it, anyway?"

"Eight o'clock. Time to rise and shine."

"You sound like my dad."

"Sorry to call so early but I'm getting ready to go flying. It's a little difficult to make a phone call from an airplane."

"That's OK, it's more than a little difficult for me to wake up in the morning," I told him. "But I appreciate the offer; I'll be ready for work at 4:30. I have to punch in at five o'clock." I figured an extra 15 minutes to spend with Matt before work was only fair.

"Great. See you then, Maggie."

"Wait!" I shouted before he could hang up on me. "What's this about a surprise?" Along with the rest of me, my curiosity was beginning to awaken.

"Can't tell you. It's a surprise, remember? Gotta run, Maggie," he teased.

After we hung up, I leaned over to the flower vase atop my nightstand

and stuck my nose up against the nearest bud. Soft and delicate petals of red velvet caressed my face as I inhaled deeply the romantic scent.

Naturally the day just dragged by. I called Bren to tell her how her wild predictions had all come true: Matt *did* explain everything to my satisfaction, he *did* like me, and he *did* ask me to go out Saturday night, even though I had to say no.

"If I didn't know better, I'd say the guy likes you," she kidded. But she seemed kind of distracted and so I let her get off the phone without telling her about the roses or that we planned to go flying together soon.

At last, it was almost time for Matt to pick me up; half a dozen outfits later, I was ready.

Matt was right on time, and although he had a lot to tell me about the sights he and his uncle had seen while flying that day, nothing was said nor was there any evidence of any kind of surprise. Matt looked the same as usual; so did his pickup. And there were no mysterious sacks or boxes to be seen. Not wishing to seem overly greedy or anxious, I didn't bring the subject up.

As we got close to Farland's, Matt looked at his watch and said, "We've got time for a quick little detour."

Aha, here it comes, I thought to myself. But ten minutes later, I was more worried about my job than some nebulous surprise.

"Matt, I'm going to be inexcusably late for work if you don't turn around this very minute."

"Can't," he said, grinning widely.

"Matt! Have you flipped? Get me to work right now. I'm serious!"

"I'm serious too," he said, still playful. "Serious about you!"

"You're hopeless," I told him.

"My mother says the same thing." I gave him an agonizing look of desperation, but instead of turning around, he pulled over to the curb and parked the truck.

"OK, time for your surprise. First of all, Mrs. MacDonald knows all about it, so don't worry about getting in trouble at work."

"Mrs. MacDonald? She's in on this too?" I couldn't believe it. What was going on?

"Well, she is now. I'll explain later. Right now, I've got to blindfold you."

"What!"

"Come on, be a good sport, Maggie. This is part of the surprise."

I let him tie the scarf over my eyes and then the truck started moving again, which gave me an eerie, helpless felling. I tried to keep a mental record of all our turns but decided that that idea only works in the movies.

When we finally came to a complete stop again, Matt told me to wait for him to come around to help me out. This part I liked; he held onto both of my hands while I jumped to the ground, and then with an arm around my waist, he guided me safely along the sidewalk.

We turned to the right, went up two steps, and then I heard a door open and some hushed whispers. Matt helped me step over the threshold without tripping. I heard the click of a light switch and knew that someone had darkened the room because until then, there had been cracks of light coming underneath the blindfold along each side of my nose.

"OK, Maggie, I'm going to take the blindfold off now," said Matt, his voice full of suppressed excitement.

As the scarf fell from my face, the lights sprang back on and a room full of kids shouted, "Surprise!" I recognized Bren's house in a second and then there she was, reaching out to hug me.

"Didn't I tell you Matt had plans for you tonight?" she said, laughing triumphantly over their successful conspiracy.

A huge sign strung across the stairway banister read "Happy Birthday, Sweet Sixteen!" At least half the Board members, most with a date, were present, as well as some of the kids from Speech 101, such as Sissie ("Gossip") Hornell, Marty Gordon, and even Harold Brenski, who proudly introduced me to his date, a girl from another school who wore the same kind of thick-lensed, plastic-rimmed glasses as Harold. In fact, she looked enough like him to be his sister, making a number of kids suspicious that

Harold had brought his own sister rather than come to a boy-girl party dateless.

"I can't believe this," I told Bren, Matt, and Randy. "How long have you guys been planning this?"

"From the time you canceled our plans for your party," answered Bren. "Remember the math problems you caught Matt and me working on at our locker? That was the guest list we were going over!"

"No wonder you seemed so nervous."

"Bren, Randy, and I decided to give you the birthday party you deserved but were too depressed to want," said Matt.

"You forgot about Carol's contribution," Randy told Matt with a sly grin.

"Carol helped with *my* party?" I asked them incredulously.

Bren looked at Matt, Matt looked at Randy, and then they both looked back at Bren who giggled, turned to me, and said, "Yes, actually, she's performing a very indispensable service tonight."

"We had all the angles covered but one," said Matt. "Our plans almost fell apart when we realized that so many girls on the Board had asked for the night off to attend your party that you were going to be the only one who couldn't come. So Carol called Mrs. MacDonald today and volunteered to take your shift."

"Carol did that for me?"

"Well," answered Bren, "for you and for the date with David King that I promised to arrange."

So now Carol would add a rock-and-roll star to her collection. I thought about how ironic it was that Carol had inadvertently given me the most valuable gift of all—the opportunity to attend my own party.

After cake and ice cream, I looked around at all the friends I'd made in two short years—including my newest friend, who sat close beside me—and decided that life wasn't as viciously unfair as I sometimes liked to believe.

Sure, losing my mother was a difficult blow to overcome. But she loved me a lot and that love will stay with me forever. Cherub's untimely death renewed past sorrows but also strengthened my ability to cope with tough times.

And now it looked as though even Dad could look forward to a bright future. He and Ann were spending more and more time together and seemed a perfect match.

A compelling desire to let all my Alaskan friends know how much I appreciated their thoughtfulness overcame me. Moving fast, before the magic of the moment could disappear, I climbed up onto a chair and called for everyone's attention.

"This is, without a doubt, the best surprise of my entire life. Believe me, everybody, I'll never forget my 16th birthday! Thank you."

Everybody clapped and cheered. I felt like joining in with them when I realized I'd just given an impromptu thank-you speech without a second thought or a single stutter!

Bren herded the party down to the basement where we could push back all the furniture and crank up the music. After a few fast dances, Matt personally supervised the selection of a slow song. Not because of my little toe, that had quit hurting days ago, but simply because he wanted to be next to me.

As Matt and I swayed gently to the music of a love song, he asked, "Well, Maggie, how do you like your suprise so far?"

"I love it, all of it!"

"There's more."

"Can't be. I'm already overwhelmed."

"Maggie, my girl, tomorrow I'm going to have the supreme privilege and pleasure of showing you the real meaning of the word."

I looked at Matt's beaming face and realized that at last I knew him well enough to know that he could be referring to only one thing.

"Flying? We're going flying tomorrow?"

"How'd you like to see your favorite glacier from the air? We could time it so our return flight coincides with the setting sun. You've never seen a sunset until you've seen one from the air."

The boy was definitely after my heart! I stole a glance over Matt's shoulder just in time to catch Bren's wink. I had no doubt who the little birdie was who had told Matt about my weakness for sunsets.

I smiled back at Matt lovingly, deciding that my 17th year of life was going to be great. After all, at last I no longer had to worry about when the right time and the right boy would come along. The right boy was Matt and our time was now.